Empower

Publishing

Also, by Percy Kepfer, M.D.
and *Empower Publishing*

The Daughter of the General

Symbiosis

The Smell of Power

by Percy Kepfer, M.D.

A Homeless Veteran

By

Percy D. Kepfer, M.D.

Empower Publishing
Winston-Salem

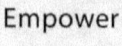

Empower

Publishing

Empower Publishing
302 Ricks Drive
Winston-Salem, NC 27103

First Empower Publishing Books edition published November, 2024
Empower Publishing, Feather Pen, and all production designs are trademarks.

For information regarding bulk purchases of this book, digital purchases and special discounts, please get in touch with the publisher at publish.empower.now@gmail.com

Cover design by Pan Morelli Manufactured in the United States of America

ISBN 978-1-63066-605-7

Dedication:

to all veterans and law enforcement officers.

—Percy D. Kepfer, MD

Chapter 1
THE VETERAN

Vincenso Batagliari, best known by his friends and family as Vince or Vic Batagliari was lying on the lawn in front of the US Capitol that morning, like most mornings for the last three or four months, ever since he became homeless. He was using his backpack as a pillow.

Most of the time, he was thinking about his life, his situation, and his future, and most importantly, whether today may be the lucky day when he would be able to approach a congressman or Congresswoman, especially if that was one in charge of veteran affairs or defense, and obviously willing to listen to him.

Vince, however, was not picky. He was fine with settling for any Congressman or woman who was willing to listen to him.

Batagliari had spent the fall and winter in this same area, waiting, thinking, and pondering. He hardly remembered when exactly he got to DC or if he had come from New York, Jersey, or Jail. His thoughts were confusing, and his mind tended to play tricks on him more often than he would like.

He knew, however, that that was why he was here, waiting.

It was now early spring, and the Japanese Cherry trees were beginning to blossom. The trees—about 3000 of them—had been gifted to Washington DC, in 1912 by the mayor of Tokyo, Yukio Ozaki, as a token of goodwill between the two countries. No one could foresee back then that 29 years later, the Japanese would be showering bombs at our fleet in Pearl Harbor Hawaii or that 100 years later they would become, again our friends and allies.

Batagliari often thought about that and could not help but compare such situations with those that occur among families, siblings, and spouses.

Batagliari was also, for the thousandth time, pondering not only the reasons why he was there but also why he became a homeless man and what "they" had done to him.

Why was "that thing" happening to him and ruining his life? Could it be stopped, and how?

Batagliari knew that someone in the US military had the answers to those questions, but no one wanted to tell him the truth for some unknown reason.

At the vet's hospitals, he was told by the Doctors that he was suffering from PSD and was given all kinds of mind-altering medications that had not helped at all, so he had to stop taking them and also stop going to the vet's clinics altogether.

He had seen the woman with the bright green dress walking fast on Pennsylvania avenue towards the Capitol building and saw her starting to climb the stairs at the front of the building and then saw her turning around and running down and away from the Capitol, as three men in dark suits were coming down from the Capitol and towards her, apparently with their weapons drown.

Vic could not see clearly if those were firearms or Taser guns, but it was clear that the woman was terrified as she ran across the street right to the spot where he was lying.

As he had many times before, Vince mentally told himself repeatedly that whatever was going on was none of his business and that whatever problem that woman had had nothing to do with him.

Common sense told him that he should not intervene in other people's problems, that he had many issues of his own, and that he could get in trouble with the law again if he intervened. But it was no use. "That thing" inside his brain made him spring into action.

So, after the woman, who was not only scared but running out of breath ran past beside him, with one of the dark suits less than twenty feet behind her, Vince just stretched his right arm and grabbed the leg of the first man, making him fall face down on the grass and letting go of the Taser gun he was holding and making is simple for Vince to shock him with it.

Vince then, tased the second man and put the third one out of commission with a Karate chop to the side of the neck.

Vince took the Taser guns, except for one, all and all the firearms and all the radio transmitters from the men, and as he ran, he disassembled them, threw it all in the closest garbage bin he found and kept walking

The woman had stopped to catch her breath and looked at Vince, surprised and incredulous at that bearded and longhaired man, dressed in old, faded, and ripped camouflage fatigues, had put down not only one, not two, but three government agents.

Vince ran towards her and, grabbing her arm, said, "I am getting out of here, sister, those suits are government agents. I do not know what you have done, but I want to stay out of it. Here, take this, maybe you will need to use it again," Vince said giving her the Taser gun and walking at a fast pace away from the Capitol and from the woman in the green dress.

He heard her running behind him and yelling, "Stop, mister, please stop.... I need help.... They may kill me!"

Without stopping, Vic responded: "If that is what they want to do, they would have used real guns, not tasers, nevertheless, I will be in a lot of shit if we get caught, so you better get out of here and away from me fast."

Vic barely heard her voice when she grabbed his arm and said, "Please help me; they are going to kill me. I do not know what to do; I am terrified; please help me. For the love of God, please help me!" The woman was sobbing uncontrollably now.

"Please, I see you are a veteran. If you still love the country you fought for, you must help me. I know something extremely important regarding national security and I have the proof here." She said this while showing him a black flash drive.

Vic's common sense alerted him, one time more to walk away, stay away from this woman, stay away from trouble, however, this time it was not "that thing" which made him say, "Okay, come with me."

It was curiosity and the feeling that perhaps that small

9

flash drive could be the key to opening a door that would allow him to talk to someone powerful enough to figure out what was causing "that thing" to happen to him.

So, getting an old camouflage jacket from his backpack, he threw it over her shoulder. "Put this on top of that dress. That color can be spotted from a mile away. This is old but clean and big enough that your fluorescent green won't show much. We are going to my place…for now."

Mentally, she questioned where he was taking her, but she thought it best not to ask and simply follow Vincenso Batagliari; somehow, this dark-haired, bearded man inspired her confidence and trust.

As if reading her thoughts, Vince said: "We are going to a place where no one will be looking for you, and then you can tell me your story… and disappear. Those suits will be up and after us in less than ten minutes, so better hurry".

By then, they had left the manicured lawn of the mall and were walking at a fast pace under the trees on the left until they reached 4th Street and then Independence Avenue towards the Smithsonian Metro Station. "I hope you have money, tokens, or a pass, because I am short of cash at the moment," Vince said. "Otherwise, we will have to jump over the fence."

The woman shook her head. She was not carrying a purse, and her dress did not have pockets, so she had no money, credit cards, or tokens.

"Shit," Vic thought; it is not very likely that this woman, in high heels and obviously expensive dress, was going to be able to jump over the metal fence or the revolving gate at the Metro station. therefore, when they got to it, Vince picked her up and, raising her above the rail, apparently with no effort, tossed her to the other side; then he simply backed up a few feet, ran, and jumped over the fence, so effortlessly as if that was something he routinely did… which actually was true.

She landed on her rump but rose quickly and unhurt, more concerned about lowering her skirt than the obviously painful area of her butt that hit the concrete of the station.

Vic could not help to notice that the woman, although

somewhat past her prime, had a gorgeous pair of legs, but never mind that he was a married man. However; a man is still a man, specially an Italian man.

Brushing his sinful thoughts away, Vince took her hand to help her get up. Then, without letting go of her hand, she dragged her after him to catch the train headed towards the Lincoln Memorial.

Getting off the Metro train there, they comfortably mixed with the large crowds of tourists visiting the site. They walked casually along Constitution Avenue, eventually reaching E. Street NW, between 20th and 21st Street.

The street's sidewalks were crowded on both sides with camping tents, army tents, makeshift tents, and an occasional cardboard dwelling, extending for at least two street blocks.

Men, women, and even a few children stood around or poked their heads from inside the dwellings as they approached. Most seemed to recognize Vince and either waved to him or simply nodded, indicating that he was recognized and given a pass into their mist.

Pedestrians, on the other hand, either avoid the street or walk in the middle of the road, risking being run over by cars which, instead of slowing down, speed up as they drove along the blocks of the street occupied by the homeless.

There were makeshift fires and even occasional Coleman gas stoves in front of some of the dwellings, and the strong smell of food, mixed with the smell of sweat, urine, and misery. "Welcome to Foggy Bottom also known as Tiny Tent Town, home of some of the Homeless, men, women and children, who barely survive in the Capital of the richest and most prosperous country in the world."

Then, stopping in front of a blue camping tent, Vic opened the tent's zipper and said to the woman, "Welcome to my mansion. Please feel free to come in, and don't be afraid of these people here. Most are my friends, and others do not even know they exist, but we all protect each other's bodies and property."

Vincenso Batagliari's tent was a little bigger than most made to accommodate 4 or 5 People for a few nights on a camping trip but certainly not made to be anybody's permanent residence.

Before entering, Vince extended his hand and said to the woman, "How rude of me! Allow me to introduce myself, Vincenso Batagliari. And you are...?"

The woman hesitated before answering, but noticing that he was looking at her directly in the eyes, with those black penetrating eyes of his, she sensed that lying to this strange, obviously handsome (when cleaned and shaved) homeless man was useless, especially since her picture and name had been so often on public media. So she eventually whispered, "It is Kelly, Kelly Carter."

It was obvious to her that he immediately recognized the name, but he did not make any comment except for a gesture showing her inside and saying, "Okay, Ms. Carter, let's hear your story while I make some coffee."

Chapter 2
A FAMILY OF WARRIORS

Although Vic felt like it had happened centuries before, in reality, it had been less than five years since he left his family home in the Bronx to join the Army.

Vincenso Batagliari did not want to join the Army, or any branch of the armed forces for that matter, he was a pacifist who wanted to be a lawyer and play the saxophone, guitar or piano. However, since, unfortunately for him , he came from a military family, it would have hurt his father deeply if he refused to serve. His father was a retired four star General, a Korean and Vietnam war veteran; his grandfather was a WWII veteran, his great-grandfather a WWI veteran in the Italian army and, according to his father stories, every male member of the Batagliari family had served in an army going as far back in time as to when Roman legions ruled the world and his ancestors were part of those legions.

Most of Vince's uncles and cousins, even the women, had been in one branch or another of the military. For goodness's sake, even his friken, ugly cousin Angelina was flying F-16s for the Air Force, making the Batagliari family extremely proud of her.

When the mothers or wives of the children objected to their boys being enrolled in the military and worried about them being killed or wounded, the Batagliari elders boasted very proudly that although many of their ancestors had been wounded in battle, none had been disabled, and none had been killed.

In fact, General Batagliari claimed that the family name Batagliari meant "Battle hero" or "Glorious warrior" in the ancient Latin language. Vic was never able to confirm this, but the General was sure that his family members were immune to being killed in battle.

Nevertheless, Vincenso Batagliari did not want to follow

the family tradition and join the armed forces. Being aware, however, that refusing to serve would hurt his father's pride and honor, very. deeply and realizing that his refusal would have literally broken his father's heart. His father had already been diagnosed with serious coronary artery disease that, in spite of a triple coronary artery bypass, had led to severe heart failure and to his early retirement from the Army. Therefore, like most Italian children, Vincenso Batagliari decided that family comes first, so he put away his dreams and joined the army to please his papa.

Nevertheless, his plan was to perform so poorly that he would be discharged after only a few weeks of basic training. This would not be too difficult since he had never been very muscular, coordinated, or good in sports

Vincenso Batagliari was considered tall for an Italian at almost 6 feet, but skinny as a rod, he only weighed about 165 pounds. His bushy, abundant, and curly black hair, which he had almost always unkempt, made him look taller, and his black eyes, above the typical Italian nose, made him look very handsome.

So, Vincenso Batagliari kept the family tradition and joined the Army, not only because that was the branch of the armed forces where his father had served but also because he believed that the Marine Corps training was more challenging. His choice did not matter to the Batagliari family, as members had served in almost every armed forces branch.

Vincenso Batagliari's grandfather—Brigadier General Vito Batagliari—had served in the Italian Army and fought in World War I from 1914 to 1928 when Italy was on the side of the US and their allies. When Benito Mussolini came to power in 1925, he was one of his many admirers and supporters until he took part in the Italian invasion and occupation of Ethiopia. After observing the atrocities committed against the Ethiopian people and the close ties of Italy with Nazi Germany, he had a change of heart.

Being well-known and respected among the military and civilian governments, it was not difficult for him to obtain a position as a military attaché at the Italian Embassy in Washington. As things began to get more serious in Europe, and after moving his family to the US, Vito Batagliari obtained asylum in the US and eventually became a US citizen.

When World War II erupted, Vito was too old to join the fighting forces, but he worked as an advisor to the US military on matters concerning Italy and Ethiopia.

Two of his three sons joined the armed forces: one served in the Marines, another in the Army Air Corps; both returned alive and untouched and received medals for their combat performance.

The youngest son of Vito Batagliari, Franklyn Vincenso Batagliari (Frankie), Vince's father, was US-born and named in honor of President Franklyn Delano Roosevelt. He and his younger sister Maria were still too young to enroll.

Frankie Batagliari did inherit the family's lust for military service. Being smart and a straight-A student, he was able to be admitted to West Point, graduated with honors, volunteered to combat service in Korea as a young cadet, and later served in Southeast Asia during the Vietnam War. Eventually, he earned a grade of general and was only forced to partially retire after he had a myocardial infarction, leading to coronary bypass surgery.

During family reunions, and after few glasses of wine, and careful about being overheard by his papa, Vince would often tell his older brothers and cousin that there were no heroes on his family, only a bunch of bloodthirsty bastards, after which they horsed around and tell him that he better soon become one of those "bloodthirsty bastards."

In any event, Vince said goodbye to his family, kissed his high school sweetheart, leaving her with a promise that he would come back and marry her and left for the nearest army training camp.

A couple of weeks after he joined, and very possibly due to his efforts to fail, one day during training, while running an obstacle course at full speed, he failed to duck on time and hit the wood beam square in the middle of his forehead, losing consciousness immediately.

And thereafter strange and suspicious things start happening to Vince Batagliari.

He woke up three days later at an Army hospital in Boston, where doctors kept putting wires on his head and running scans and other tests. Thereafter, after a couple of weeks in the hospital, and much to his surprise, instead of being discharged—as he learned later should have been the normal and proper procedure after suffering a serious cerebral concussion—not only was he sent back to basic training but assigned to a special forces unit. His father was around most of the time while he was in the hospital, but neither his girlfriend nor his mother were allowed to visit until he had a day off, the day before they marched him to the new training camp.

Neither his father nor the doctors gave him a straight answer about what had happened to him except to assure him that "everything was all right" and that he was "as good as new." And, of course, in response to his questions about whether or not he was going to be discharged, the standard answer was "of course not; you are now better than new."

Soon he found out that, at least about the last part, the physicians and his father had been correct. He felt better, stronger and more focused. He was now able to run faster than his peers, climb the obstacle courses almost effortlessly and be unbeaten in hand-to-hand combat. He however did not feel totally normal. As far as being himself, he felt that he was changed in mind and body. Although he still did not like being in the Army, the fact that he was doing so well on his training encouraged him to keep going, especially now that he did not have an excuse for failing.

However, he had nightmares and difficulty controlling his temper. In fact, the first time that "that thing" happened, he was almost at the end of basic training when he saw a drill sergeant belittle and hit a young, enlisted boy who obviously was too feeble to complete the task assigned to him.

As the boy fell on the ground and the sergeant was about to kick him, something snapped in Vince's head, he felt a rush of adrenaline and before he could even think about it he was punching the drill sergeant in the middle of the face, hearing the crack of a broken nose. He spent two weeks in the stockade, but once again was not expelled from the Army. Doctors and psychiatrists came to see him often, and more tests were run. Eventually, he went to special training and to Iraq and Afghanistan, where he had several episodes of "that thing", which were actually helpful to his unit and made him a war hero and earner of a Medal of Honor.

However, after several tours of duty and three long years, he was due to be discharged. Since his father heart had finally failed for good, Vince saw no reason to re-enroll and returned to civilian life, having married his sweetheart a year earlier.

The transition was not easy, however. Although it was easy for Vince to find jobs, he did not last in them, mostly due to his bad temper and conflicts with his coworkers, superiors, or clients, which occasionally led to physical confrontations and involvement with the police.

Two of the most serious events occurred in New York, one in the subway. He was riding back home after work when three punks were harassing an old black man, and one of them pulled a knife trying to rob him. Vince felt "the thing." He sprung to action. Before he knew it, he had broken the arm of one of the young thugs, stabbed one in the leg with his own knife, and broken the nose of the third when the police arrived. The thugs accused him of assaulting them without reason. Vincent, being still angry, punched one of the cops. He spent a few days in jail for the assault on the cop, but the Judge dismissed the charges of assaulting the punks, and the cop, having been an Army man himself, withdrew those charges.

But then there were the nightmares and the fights at home, mostly due to his bad temper, inability to hold a job, and lack of money, causing the wife to have to work two jobs and leave their two young girls with Vince's mother, most of the time.

The end came after the Home Depot job. The family knew the manager, and Vince was doing well for about 3 months until the day when an irate customer insulted one of Vince's coworkers and threw a heavy piece of board at her, hitting her in the leg.

The "thing" made Vince jump, grab the guy by the neck, pin him to the ground and start punching him until three or four people pulled them apart. The guy ended up in the hospital and Vince in jail.

This time the judge sent him to prison for a year. He was released after six months, with him to this day not being sure why. It was not for good behavior because he got into fights and broke a few noses while there. Doctors from the Veterans hospital came to see him, interviewing and testing and probably it was because of them that he was released early because of a "mental condition", "likely Post Traumatic Stress Disorder."

Unfortunately, when he returned home, his wife left with the two girls and moved in with her parents. When Vince tried to get her back, he found out that both she and the girls were scared of him. Worse, during the conversation with his wife, things got heated, words were said, and he, once again, almost got physical, causing his in-laws to call the police and to be arrested again, this time for resisting arrest.

After his release from jail, Vince decided a few things: first, his wife was right, he was unpredictable and, second, he was afraid to cause harm to his loved ones, and therefore, as much as he loved them he had to leave. Third, these problems started after he was hospitalized for the head injury. He decided the doctors had to have done something to his brain. Therefore, he needed to find out who and what they had done to him.

Then, he had to learn to control "that thing".

"Shit, those fucking doctors made me into a friken Incredible Hulk. But even the Hulk eventually learned to control his rage. So will I. Thank God I do not have the strength of the Hulk."

So, he moved out of his home collecting only a fraction of his Disability Pension and sending the rest to his wife, but soon he found out that this small amount was not enough to pay for a room and food, so he joined the Homeless.

The doctors at the VA in Boston and Washington did not have, or did not want to give him any answers, insisting that what he had was PTSD and prescribed pills. He was convinced that he had been the victim of some government experiment, for which, sadly enough, his own father probably consented, and he was dead now. Therefore, the only possible way to find out was through a Congressperson with enough influence to request and investigate his case. The biggest problem was to find someone willing to listen and believe him, so far, he had not been fortunate, and lately he was not even let into the Capitol building due to his shabby appearance.

As far as being able to control "that thing", he was working on it—working very hard indeed, and so far, he had been able only to control the intensity and henceforth, the seriousness of the damage that he would cause to the person or persons he attacked.

Vince Batagliari said to himself, "At least that is something; a beginning, and I am not turning green yet."

Chapter 3
THE LADY IN THE GREEN DRESS

The woman was nervous, frightened and uneasy. It was clear that she did not know if she should trust this raggedy young man who lived in a tent in the middle of the Capital City of the United States, but she felt that she had no choice. So, she took a sip of coffee from the cup that the homeless man had handed to her. It was a tin cup, the kind that you take while camping, but it appeared to be clean, and the coffee smelled good. She hesitated but then looking at the man directly in the eye and finding it reassuring she began, "I am Kelly Carter, the press secretary of the President of the United States…or most likely I used to be the Press Secretary of the President of the United States until earlier this morning… as I am now, very sure that I lost the job."

She paused, took another sip of coffee, and continued, "This morning I went to work as usual, and after the briefing, everyone left the conference room with the exception of the President, the Vice-President, a couple of generals, and me.

"Then, the Secretary of State walked in to the room with few other people, among them a man and a woman that I knew have seen before. The woman was the most familiar, but I also had seen the man before, he was oriental, either Chinese or Korean. The President looked a bit annoyed because of my presence in the room, and he did not introduce the newcomers to me, which I considered unusual. Then she asked me to leave the room and wait outside, again, something unusual.

"Needless to say, this pricked my curiosity some. Instead of carrying my laptop with me, I left it open, turned the microphone on, casually dropped it on a chair, and left the room. After I left, I went to my office and turned my desktop computer and connected it to my laptop."

"So, all of a sudden, you decided to spy on the President

of the United States?" said Vince.

Another pause, another sip of coffee, and Kelly responded obviously offended.

"No, it was not that way. It was only curiosity. I never meant to record what I heard onto a flash drive until I realized that the subject of the conversation amounted to treason and compromised national security. I am an American. I owe loyalty to my country before I own loyalty to the president.

"Evidently not everyone knew everyone, as there were introductions. Unfortunately, they exchanged names before I started recording. However, I believe some were CEOs of big pharma.

"The woman I know was/is a doctor from Walter Reed Hospital, a researcher. Her name is Lidia Del Toro, and the oriental guy, I did not know who he was but I remember his name, as it struck me as funny. It was something like Doctor Chin-Gan-Do, and it seems this guy and Dr. Lidia work together.

"What they were saying is that Scientists at Walter Reed, under the direction of those two doctors have altered the DNA of a virus that they isolated from bats, and had made it very infectious and lethal to humans.

"It was very frightening. They were talking about sending this virus to China with this doctor and, with the consent of the Chinese government, release the virus into the population. They were going to create an epidemic of monumental proportions while temporarily withholding a vaccine, that the Chinese already have developed, to neutralize the virus, until enough people have died in China and elsewhere to force people to pay any price for such vaccine.

"Someone said that the virus would make young people only mildly ill, but it would be lethal to most elderly individuals and those people who suffer from chronic diseases."

Kelly stopped once more and took another sip of coffee before continuing her story.

"At some point, someone in the room, I believe a doctor from one of the drug companies, expressed his concern that a

21

new virus with such enormous power, once released will be difficult, if not impossible, to control, and even if such thing was possible. Thousands, perhaps millions of people could die meanwhile. I am a Christian and a physician. My training was to save lives, not to kill. Sorry, but I do not want any part of this.

"Another person, I think one of the generals, also expressed his disapproval, stating that he had been sworn to defend this country and its people, regardless or skin color, race or age and that what they were talking about there was nothing less than genocide. It appears that, at this point, he got up and left the room.

"To this, the woman doctor responded that those people targeted by the virus were older and already sick and probably be going to die sooner than later and that their departure from this world would be highly beneficial to taxpayers because billions would be saved from Social Security payments, Medicare, Medicaid, and other insurances.

"It sounded to me that most people in the room, except those two, agreed. Then they discussed details and the staggering number of billions this homemade virus would generate for each of the pharmaceutical corporations and insurance companies they represented. It seemed to me that their main concern was that the Chinese government requested sixty percent and the Americans forty.

"But that is not all. Our government was to pretend to be horrified if someone ever disclosed that the Chinese had released the virus intentionally and would mobilize our military into full alert, while the Chinese would do the same with their forces. Of course, the whole thing would be nothing but a smoke screen; nevertheless, concerns were raised that something could go wrong with this scenario and get us into a full-scale war with the Chinese.

"Needless to say, I was horrified and flabbergasted; I could not believe my ears; I am an American; I am a patriot. Therefore, at some point during that exchange, I put a flash drive and started recording. I am not exactly sure when and have no idea of how much was recorded. All I know is that someone in the conference room saw my laptop and called it to the attention of the President, who sent for the Secret Service to find out where or if it was connected to an outside source.

"At this point, I panicked, turned off my desktop computer, put the flash drive in my pocket, and tried to leave my office. I was stopped by an agent who asked me if I was aware that I left my laptop in the conference room. Of course, I lied, pretending that I just had noticed that, but I could tell that he did not believe me and asked me if I had heard any of the conversations that the president was having with his staff. I told him I had full clearance at the White House, but he reminded me that the President had asked me to leave the conference room.

"I panicked more; my hands were sweating, and I know those guys are trained to detect those things in people they interrogate, so I told him that his questions were making me uncomfortable and that I needed to use the restroom.

"He told me to go ahead; meanwhile they were going to check the tapes from the security cameras in my office. I did not even know that they had those there.

"So, I went to the restroom, exited another way, and ran out, hoping to reach the Capitol building and tell my story to any representative or senator willing to listen to me.

"You know the rest," she finished.

"So, basically, you do not know what part of all that is in your flash drive; I guess we better look at it before we go looking for a congressman or woman. There is an Internet Café nearby. Let's go there."

The internet café was almost deserted at that time, and the few people there hardly paid any attention to them. Vince paid the attendant for half an hour of computer, with coins that he had in a tin can at his tent and Kelly inserted the flash drive.

After the computer screen came to life and they both listened, it was mostly static, but there were some clear sounds and parts of pictures. One could see the president, the vice president, other men in civilian clothes and two generals in uniform. The voice of a woman, most likely Doctor Toro, was heard explaining the savings on Medications, Medicare, Medicaid and Social Security with this new development. The word virus was not heard, and only the part about having the military ready for China was heard.

Nothing was really compromising on the flash drive. Kelly almost screamed, "That is not all! That is not all, at all, and those people were talking genocide on a great scale and all for profit. There should be more in that drive."

"Well, Mrs. Carter, perhaps there is, but that static scrambles it," said Batagliari. I do believe you; however, I am not an important politician. I hope some of them believe you, too. And let's hope that someone there has some way to unscramble that flash drive."

As they were about to turn the computer off the screen of a television set hanging from the wall flashed the news

"BREAKING NEWS"

"The White House reported this afternoon with great concern and regret that one of the most trusted staffers of the present administration, none other than Mrs. Kelly Carter, the press secretary of the President, suffered this morning a serious nervous breakdown, became delusional and violent, attacking three members of the Secret Service who tried to control her.

"Thereafter she ran hysterically from the White House and to this moment her whereabouts are unknown.

"Since she does not have any known previous history of mental problems, experts speculate that she may have taken some hallucinogenic drug.

"The White House security service, otherwise known as the Secret Service, will investigate. However, as of the time of this report, Mrs. Carter's whereabouts are unknown.

"There are speculation that she may be wandering around, lost in the city, as she seemed to have developed a temporary memory loss and may not be able to recognize time or place.

"The President, the White House staff, and Mrs. Carter's husband are very concerned. Therefore, we ask the citizens to call the police if they happen to see this lady."

A picture of her appeared on the screen after the news bulletin.

"They cannot do this shit to me," Kelly almost shouted, now nobody will believe me."

The TV reporter was still broadcasting the news about Kelly when he switched gears and almost screamed.

"IN OTHER BREAKING NEWS"

"The well-known physician Dr. Christian Shaw, head investigator of Pfizer Corporation, was tragically killed in a fiery automobile accident about an hour ago, along with his passenger General William Bright.

"Apparently, they were driving together after leaving a conference with the President at the White House. The President and the Vice President express their sincere condolences to their families. They will both be buried at Arlington with military honors and the flag will fly at half-mast for three days in their honor, by special order of the President of the United States."

Kelly had to put her hand in front of her mouth to avoid screaming, but she said to Vince, "Do you know who those are?"

"Let me guess. Those two guys did not go along with the President's monstrous plan. Obviously, they had to be killed. Now you know what we are up against."

"We, you mean you are going to help me?"

"It seems that I do not have much choice, Mrs. Kelly. By now, I am sure they know who you are with."

"How could they know that?" responded Kelly. "You put out the guys that were chasing me, and we did not leave the park together; at some points, you were ahead of me, and at others, I was ahead of you."

"Lady, I have been a permanent feature of that park for the last four months and I am sure every spook has a picture of me. All of a sudden, I am not there. They are not stupid, and their job is to put two and two together, and trust me, not very often do they get five."

As she remained silent, Vince added,

"Here is what we have to do: first of all, let's make copies of that flash drive; second, let's find some less conspicuous clothes for you; third, we find a computer guru or a hacker who could be able to get more out of that drive, and four, you find someone you trust and has some power in this government to pass this information to."

"I think I can take care of items one, two and three. Item four would be totally up to you," Kelly responded. "But don't we need at least some money for that? No offense, but what is left in your tin can is probably only enough to buy us two happy meals at McDonald's."

"Let me take care of that. I do not have any money with me, but I have a debit card; the government deposits my veteran disability checks in my bank account. I transfer three-quarters of it to my ex-wife's account, and I am very careful as to how to spend the remaining whopping $650, so I have a small amount left in my account."

"Is that all you get for your services…$2500?"

"Whoa, I see you are good at math. Yep, that is all, 2500 greenbacks."

She remained silent and felt tremendous sorrow and guilt for that unsung hero and all others like him.

"Do not feel sorry for me, lady; I would be fine if I could be able to work or go to school. I be better….if it wasn't for what they did to me."

"Who and what was done to you; were you captured and tortured?"

"Perhaps I was but not by any enemy, but by our own people…they did something to my head in those military hospitals, and I need to find what."

"I believe you because I know now what the government is capable of, and that is why I want to help you. Perhaps we can help each other."

"Let's go back to tent city and borrow some poor people's clothes, but first, let me talk to the owner here. I'm going to try to get those flash drives on credit and find out if he knows any computer guru. The owner is from Pakistan and those guys are very good with computers; besides, he knows me. I come here about once a week to talk to my girls on the computer."

The Pakistani was nice and trustful so let them have three flash drives to copy the conversation from the Oval Office, while promising Vince that he was going to call around for a hacker; so they returned to tent city.

A young woman who looked much older than her actual age would happily trade a faded, old jogging suit for the lady's green dress.

The woman was delighted because Vince promised to return the jogging suit and told her she could keep the green dress anyway.

So, dressed in a grey, faded jogging suit and covering her head with an old Atlanta Braves baseball cap, Kelly Carter was almost impossible to recognize.

"What now?" she asked Vincenso.

"First, we go to my bank's ATM, then to Goodwill to buy you better-fitting garments, then to Wal-Mart to buy a cell phone, have a Subway sandwich, and finally call whoever you can call to report this mess and get help from him or her."

"That may be a problem, Mr. Vince, because I do not have my cell phone, my computer or my Rolodex with me and I probably would not be able to remember the phone numbers of anyone I trust to call"

"Shit...please excuses my French; can you call a friend or a colleague to get a number? If you can think of a name of a person, we can trust... don't call home or work, okay?"

"I am not that stupid, Mr. Vince; just let me think about who to call while we walk to the nearest Wal-Mart store. I am starving, too and a hoagie sandwich sounds like a great idea."

Chapter 4
THE SENATOR

Halfway through the sandwich, Kelly said, "I know what I can do. Once you get the phone, I will call my best friend Laura, who is also best friends with a cousin of a US Senator and knows almost everyone in the Senate. She may know the kind of Senator we both are looking for.

"Moreover, although the Senator I am thinking of belongs to the same party as the president, they disagree on most issues. He is a true patriot and an honest person...a rare gem these days and especially in this government, that unfortunately, I trusted and defended for so long."

Vic took a big gulp of his soda before responding, "We all make mistakes, Mrs. Carter. Unfortunately, most people don't recognize nor admit them, and worse, they not only never apologize and much less make amendments but usually justify their faults or blame someone else for them. Remember that Jesus came to save sinners, not to take saints. Can you tell me the name of this rare gem?"

"I am sure you heard of him, Mr. Vic; he is the head of the Armed Forces Committee in Congress and also a wounded, decorated hero."

"Hope you are talking about Senator James McClain. He could help my case as well."

"Yes, I will bet he could but first, we have to get his phone number and see if he is willing to listen to us"

With this, they finished their late lunch. Vince had used the ATM at the store to get some money, and after that, they shopped for a pair of jeans, a T-shirt, and sneakers, which Kelly changed into at the store's dressing rooms, keeping the Atlanta Braves cap on. Meanwhile, Vic bought a cheap cell phone, and they walked out of the store.

Then they walked back to Tent City to return the jogging suit and pay the Pakistani man; as they walked out, Kelly called her best friend Laura, eventually obtaining Senator's McClain phone number, and the numbers of few other Senators and Congresspersons, via text.

Finally, she told Vince, "My friend Laura got several Senator's home phone numbers, including Senator McClain. I also asked her to call my husband to let him know I was okay. So far, she will test the numbers back to me in a few seconds."

"Shit..." Vic said again followed with the usual "Please excuse my French. They, for sure, are tapping your husband's phone, and they will be able to trace that call. So, as soon as we get the numbers, we will get rid of that phone and call our Senator from a paid phone somewhere. Unfortunately, my limited funds do not allow me to buy several cell phones daily."

"I am sorry," she said sarcastically and somewhat hurt. "I am not too familiar with this spy game. And please be sure that I will pay you everything you have spent as soon as we leave this mess."

"If we come out of this mess, you mean. So, listen, I am sorry, Mrs. Carter. I did not mean to offend you, and you do not owe me anything; if I reacted angrily, it is just because of what they did to my head in the military."

Almost immediately, she felt sorry for the man; he was right; she had been careless. She wanted to tell him to call her Kelly instead of Mrs. Carter, but she felt that perhaps that was not the best occasion to tell him that.

Instead, she gave him the phone after she got the senator's numbers from her friend and wrote them down on a piece of paper they picked up from a garbage can.

Vic grabbed the phone without saying anything. After deleting all the messages, he tossed the phone into the bed of the truck when they spotted a pickup truck with out-of-state license plates and said, "That will give them some work to do, and us some room to breathe, for a while."

It was almost rush hour but neither of them knew if the Senator went home for dinner or even if Mrs. McClain Would be home at that hour, they decided to wait at least one hour before calling and meanwhile, they kept walking until they found themselves at L'Enfant plaza, in front of the International Spy Museum. They both laughed at the irony but since they were running out of money, could not afford to go inside.

At 6.15 pm Kelly dialed the Senator from a paid phone and was lucky enough that Mrs. Edith McClain personally picked up at the third ring.

"Edith, this is Kelly Carter. You know who I am; we met several times before. Please do not hang up. Please, listen to what I have to tell you. I do not know if you have seen the news, but if you have, do not believe it. It is all lies, and this is a matter of national security. My life is in danger, and I need to talk to your husband urgently. I do not have any money, I do not have a telephone, I am calling from a paid phone, and I am desperate. Please call your husband and tell him to call the number of this paid phone as soon as possible. Thank you and God bless you."

When Kelly gave the number, she was in tears and sobbing.

It was less than ten minutes later that the paid phone rang and Kelly jumped to answer.

It was Senator McClain.

"Senator, this is Kelly Carter, please listen to me I have an issue of maximum national security that I must communicate to you, but it is so sensitive that I cannot do it over the phone. Could it be possible for you to meet us at the McDonalds near the Spy Museum on C Street SW?"

". . . Oh, thank you, sir. Please be careful and make sure nobody is watching or following you. Perhaps if you have a bodyguard, you should bring him along."

". . . Your driver, sure, that be fine, just be extra careful"

Then she said to Vic," He is coming; he will meet us at a McDonald nearby. Let's go."

They walked to the restaurant and ordered two coffees, at a dollar a piece, after this they were left with less than ten dollars between them. Kelly was praying in low voice for the senator to show up.

About twenty minutes later he did.

Senator James McClain was a distinguished-looking man, well into his sixties but still slim and fit. His hair was white and balding, and his blue eyes had a sense of peace but also a sense of determination; at six foot tall, he was an impressive man who inspired respect but also admiration. He had been a decorated war veteran and a US senator for nearly two decades, being known for his lack of partisanship and willingness to reach across the aisle when whatever was being debated favored the people who elected him, even if it was necessary to go against the party or the President himself. He was also head of the Armed Forces committee.

McClain was followed by one of the tallest and most muscular guys Kelly had ever seen. At least seven feet tall, neatly fitted in a grey chauffer uniform, he stood at the door and let the senator walk inside.

Vic whispered at Kelly's ear, "The big guy is packing a big iron, even though he probably never needs it."

Kelly smiled and got up to meet the senator. After thanking him for coming and introducing Vince, she handled him one copy of the flash drive and told him to keep it with his life, then politely offered him a coffee. "The coffee here is actually very good, sir."

"Okay. I'll take a cup to go but we better get moving, I believe we had a tail while coming here but Jason was able to shake it. So let's go. We will have dinner at my home and you tell me all about whatever it is there. I suggest you, Kelly, get in the back of my car and keep your head down. You my friend, if you wish to tag along an it is okay with Kelly, will have to ride in the trunk.

"It is indeed a good coffee Mrs. Carter," said Senator McClain, "It has been a while since I had anything at any McDonald's. I believe last time it was when our grandkids visited us for Christmas. Now tell me how important this is you want to tell me that you call me at my home, just before dinner, present yourself in a sort of a disguise, accompanied by an unknown fellow and, if I may say so, incredibly distressed."

"Well sir, I believe that the president and his minions are planning what seems to me high treason and genocide and, because I stole the proof of it, they are most likely going to kill me".

She paused to take a sip of her coffee and continued.

"As to the man you are referring to, he saved my life this morning and he is a veteran with some very important issues of his own that he be glad to explain to you."

"Your own words, Mrs. Carter, were that "you believed that the president is up to no good; what it is that do you believe the president is done or about to do?"

"Sorry, sir, that was a poor choice of words; I KNOW FOR A FACT THAT THE PRESIDENT IS UP TO NO GOOD. The proof is in that flash drive I just gave you. And after I tell you the whole story, you see why my life is at risk and also the life of this good man who helped me."

By then it was getting dark. It was past rush hour and the restaurant was filling with customers, making it more difficult to be inconspicuous. The senator told them to get going. Kelly was to ride in the back seat of the car with the senator and lower her head or slide down to the floor of the car not to be seen. Jason was to drive around the back of the restaurant and popup the trunk for Vincent to jump into it. Once this was accomplished, they drove away.

Senator McClain did not have to tell Jason to drive straight into the garage of his home, even though it was more common for him to park the car in front of the house, in case McClain needed to get out again later, something that was more usual than not. In any event, once in the garage, Kelly got out, and then Vince came out of the trunk. They all went into the house through a door that opened directly into the kitchen.

The senator's home was elegantly decorated in old Victorian style, and some of the furniture looked old enough to be from Queen Victoria's days. It was a two-story house with a formal dining room and living room, a spacious studio and library, and a master bedroom on the first floor. Upstairs, there were at least four bedrooms with adjoining bathrooms, and below was a cellar or basement.

The Senator explained that the master bedroom used to be upstairs and there were two bedrooms for the kids downstairs. As he and his wife were getting up in years, and arthritis and other ailments started to set in, the house was remodeled and the bedrooms situation reversed.

Edith McClain was in the kitchen casually but elegantly dressed, wearing a red apron and stirring a large pot of food that smelled delicious. She washed her hands in the kitchen sink, dried them with her apron, and approached the newcomers with open arms, kissing Kelly on the cheek.

"Welcome, dear Kelly. It has been a while since the last time I saw you. How are you doing? It seems like you are in some trouble; hope we can help."

"Hope so too, Edith. It is nice to see you and thank you for keeping us in your home. Please excuse my appearance but we had a very, very hectic day."

"It sure seems that way. I have been watching the news, and I did not believe a word of what they said. And who is this handsome fellow? Is he with you?"

At his Vince step forward and said, "Please, allow me to introduce myself, Mrs. McClain, my name is Vincenso Batagliari, but you can call me Vince. I had the privilege of meeting Mrs. Carter only this morning and to be of some assistance to her."

"Italian right? . . . I was going to say that I hope you like spaghetti because after I got Kelly's call, I sent my maid home earlier than usually, so you can tell us freely your story. Spaghetti is one of the few dishes I can cook more or less well. Only now, with an Italian as a guest, I am totally afraid that my spaghetti will taste poorly to him."

"I am sure your spaghetti is the best I have ever tasted, Mrs. McClain," said Vince politely as the Senator, returning from the bathroom and said:

"Enough chat woman. These people are starving let's go eat and do not believe her, as far as I am concerned her spaghetti is the best."

It was obvious to Kelly and Vince that the Senator and

Edith McClain still had tender feelings for one another. This almost made Kelly Carter cry, as she remembered that after ten years of marriage, her husband and she rarely had any tender or complimentary words for each other . . . and no children.

After they each went to the bathroom to refresh, all five of them sat at the table. Jason, the driver and bodyguard, shared the meal with them.

Besides spaghetti, there was salad, red wine, Italian bread, coffee, and ice cream. Vince thought it was almost as good as the dishes his mother used to make and said so to Mrs. McClain, making her smile proudly.

After dinner, the senator invited Kelly and Vince to come down to the basement, where he had a small office and his computer. Jason was told to stay guard in case some uninvited guest showed up and Edith was told that perhaps it would be safer for her to ignore what was going to be discussed.

Once the guest sat on comfortable lazy boy chairs, the Senator told Vince,"So, you said that your last name is Batagliari. I served with a Batagliari in Vietnam; any relation?"

"I believe that would have been my father, sir; he arrived there with the first group, the 9th Marine Expeditionary, and stayed through most of the war. Most of my family members, even the women are or were at some point serving in the military. I served in Afghanistan. I was a Lieutenant. And there is something related to that that I would like to bring up to your attention, after you listen to the most important issue, the one that Mrs. Carter is bringing to you."

Kelly Carter told her story to the Senator from the beginning, when she saw the men going into the Oval Office up until her meeting with Vincenso and their feeling that the two men who bailed out of participating in the sinister scheme, had been assassinated.

The Senator listened carefully while sipping on a glass of brandy—that had been offered to his guests and politely refused—and then, without a word, got up and turned on a computer and inserted that copy of the flash drive that Kelly had given him. After watching the recording a couple of times, he turned around and said to them:

"Oh . . ., Mrs. Carter, I am afraid that I agreed with the Lieutenant; there is not much in this recording to confirm your story. However the fact that you said that two of the men who were on that meeting and declined to cooperate died in a freak accident just minutes after that meeting gives credibility to the whole story. It also indicates that we are all in great danger. Therefore I believe that we need to protect ourselves and the best way to do that is to make as many people aware of this plot as we possibly can."

"How many is that, Senator?" Vince inquired. He continued, "I have a friend who has a copy of the flash drive. He is trustworthy and a computer guru. He is trying to figure out if we can get more out of that drive."

"Not a very good idea to bring outsiders into this matter, Lieutenant. We probably should retrieve that copy as soon as possible. If that person is trustworthy, he may be in great danger as we speak."

"Sorry Senator, I trust my friends. They are really good at this, and I am sure that they cannot trace him this fast"

"You never know, Lieutenant. We better warn him and watch him. "

"And I just want my life back. I want to be safe. I want to be able to trust my president again. Also, I want my cell phone, my credit cards, some money, decent clothes," said Kelly tearfully, bringing a paternal smile to the normally serious face of the senator.

"I am afraid, my dear Mrs. Carter, that the first four wishes cannot be granted. The first will probably be impossible after what you saw and heard. The second and third can be a sure way to track you down. As to the fourth and fifth, I can lend you some money, and Edith can share some garments with you until we order some from Amazon.

"Let me first start the ball rolling," continued the senator, who seemed to be having a good time dealing with the situation and summoning his driver Jason.

Jason came into the room, handed the senator two

semiautomatic pistols, with four magazines for each, and holstered a third one on his belt.

The senator handled one to Vince and said, "These are just precautions we have to take, hopefully they don't know where you are. Still, I am sure they are watching everyone whom you guys may possible approach. Although, unfortunately, I belong to the same party as the president, we have never been marching at the same tune and he knows I love my country. As I told you both, we already had a tail when we left to get you at the McDonald's.

"Now, please, Lieutenant, tell Jason where he can get your computer guru, friend. He will bring him or her here."

"With all due respect, Senator, I was trained not to trust anyone, and under the circumstances, you will understand. Therefore, I prefer to get my friend personally."

Jason's facial expression did not change a bit and the big man look at the senator waiting for his response.

"Understandable, Lieutenant, understandable and commendable as well. However, you will understand that if you are seen leaving or coming into my home, we all be in danger."

"I will call my friend to meet me at the McDonald's and ride in the trunk of the car, if you want me to."

"Actually, Jason is driving his own car. You can lie down in the back seat, at least until you are certain that there is not a tail."

"Thank you, Senator; please accept my apology."

"No problem, Lieutenant, I understand perfectly. You will tell me your story when we come back. Please use Jason's spare phone to call your friend."

Vince called his Pakistani friend at the computer café and instructed him to meet him at the McDonald's by the Spy Museum. Then they entered the garage and got into Jason's black Chevy Blazer.

Chapter 4
THE PRESIDENT

His rubicund face turned even redder and puffier than usual due to his rage. His sparse blond hair, usually in disarray, was even more so, because he passed his hands through it very often as he pounded at his Oval Office desk. His eyes of a normal clear blue were now becoming reddish and dark shades were appearing under his puffy lower eyelids.

He was obese, hypertensive and borderline diabetic. Therefore, the men in the room were concerned that the president was close to having a stroke, such was the display of fury that he was demonstrating.

"Sir … I am sure that we can get this under control, all we have to do is find the woman, after all she is not the black widow of Marvel comics. She has got to be somewhere."

"Have your men checked her home, and the homes of her friends and relatives; has the Secret Service?"

"Yes sir, but you said before that you do not want them too involved, due to the secrecy and delicacy of this matter. So they were told the same story that we released to the press, stating the fact that she has in her possession a computer file that could compromise National Security," said the Vice-President.

Slightly more calm the President said, "Of course every agent involved should be instructed not to try to see what is on the drive."

"That is correct, sir… They've been instructed carefully to that effect. Besides we are not sure what is on that flash drive. We will see what is on her computers, but due to the delicacy of the subject we are not able to use any of our experts here. General Masters is bringing some of his most trusted men to help in the investigation and conduct whatever action is needed to correct this problem. I believe it is the same team that conducted the operation to erase the two dissidents from our group."

The phone of the third man in the room, a man in military uniform, rang. After answering, he informed the other men, with a grin on his face, "Good news. It seems that Mrs. Carter called a friend from a cell phone. They have located the call and are now tracking down the phone. It seems to be in a vehicle moving out of town and heading south"

The president calmed down a bit and said, "Tell them to use a helicopter and stop the vehicle. The poor woman has really gone mad…. Imagine leaving town and going south all by herself and without money or credit cards. They are all here inside this purse. Her driver's license is here, as well as her ID and clearance. Do you all think that she stole a car or is into high jacking? I can't picture Kelly stealing a car. She is most likely high jacking, but where is she going? Does she have family or close friends anywhere south of DC?

"We don't know but that should be easy to find out without blowing the secrecy of this project, which, damn you all, is already not that secret; and if we use our vast but normal resources, we may blow the lid of this and I not only be impeached but very likely go to jail—and you with me. Therefore to all of you, we are all simply concerned about the welfare of a poor and dear civil servant who, for unclear reasons, lost her mind and is wondering around somewhere, probably going south."

General Masters phoned some orders, and in less than fifteen minutes, they had the answer: Kelly's parents had moved to Fort Pierce, Florida, two years earlier after they retired and now lived a quiet life in a gated community in that town. So, he ordered to have 24-hour surveillance of their residence.

The three men calmed down, went into the bookcase on the wall and moved some fake books, showing a full bar behind it. They got glasses, poured themselves a scotch on the rocks from a decanter, and toasted to their good fortune.

That enjoyment did not last long, General Masters's phone rang again, and his ordinarily sour expression turned even sourer as he said loudly "FUCK" and turning to the president and vice-President, he informed them: "Either this woman is smarter than we think, or someone is helping her. They located the phone. It was thrown in the back of a pickup truck going south. The driver did not even know it was there until the police stopped him. The good news is they have the phone and will soon be able to tell who she made calls to.

"Gentlemen, I believe it is time to get dirty. I am going to mobilize my team and deal with this lady and whoever is helping her personally. I hope that it is not too late to stop this mess from getting messier. I'll have Leopold and his team, as well as my men deal with this. They are smart, have the electronics, the expertise, and the guts."

As he said that, the laptop computer and the desktop computer that belonged to Kelly Carter came to life, eliciting a loud and synchronous "Shit" from all three men.

Chapter 5
HACKERS

As Senator McClain was taking the last sip of his brandy, they heard his driver's car pull into the garage. Vince, Jason, and two men wearing hoods over their heads walked into the room.

Jason said apologetically, "I thought that it would be safer to bring Mr. Batagliari's friends this way; you never know who to trust these days. Unfortunately, Mr. Batagliari did not agree with me on this matter, and I am afraid we had a little confrontation. Fortunately, I was able to convince him of the need for such measures."

It was not until then that the Senator and Kelly Carter noticed the swollen faces of both men.

The senator chuckled, saying, "I am glad you prevailed using your strong arguments."

"Actually, sir, Mr. Batagliari was prevailing, but the words of his friends convinced him that it was best if we hooded them, both for our security and ours."

"Very good then. So, before we remove the hoods, let me kill the lights of this room and go behind my desk lamp, to keep things more private. Please refrain from use real names or titles. Did you have any other problem? Were you followed?"

"There is a car with spooks parked across the street from us but they are just watching the house, and you, sir. They did not bother to follow us."

"Great. Let's take the hoods of the heads of these two good men, with my apologies for the inconvenience."

After doing that with the room mostly in the dark, except the area where the two hooded men, Jason and Vince were, the hoods were removed. Vince introduced the men as Mr. Ahmed Patel, a very good friend and owner of the internet café where Vince went weekly to talk cybernetically with his daughters, and his cousin Babar Patel, both from Pakistan and now legal US citizens. "They both are what we consider computer experts or computer gurus. Both have seen the flash drive and worked on it. Unfortunately, there is no more on it than what we have seen already."

"Then why do we need them, Mr. Vince?" asked the senator from the shade.

"We needed them because they tell me that it may be possible to hack into Mrs. Carter's computers, the ones she left at the White House. And I believe they can. They are good at this computer thing," responded Vince.

"Okay, I am willing to let them try, although by now, those computers are likely undergoing a most detailed revision or may be destroyed," stated the Senator.

"Perhaps, but Jason and I think that due to the very delicate subject, this situation is not going to be handled by the CIA, the FBI, or any legal agency because those could land them in jail. We believe they will assemble a special team of some sort and, since this was a totally unexpected twist in the plot, that will take them some time. First, they would want to know how much of the conversation that took place this morning was copied on the computers."

"Therefore, they need people like Mr. Patel and Mr. Babar to unscramble it, and it had to be people working under the radar, not official government employees," Kelly Carter said from the back of the room. "I suppose that you gentlemen need my password in order to do that, right?"

"Not really Mrs. C, we can get in without knowing your password, but it will sure save us some valuable time if we have it."

After Kelly gave them the password, Babar sat in front of the computer while his cousin asked Jason to fetch some electronic equipment from the car.

The senator asked the two hackers if they wanted a drink, and they said they would like some tea. After a few minutes, the senator told Kelly and Vince to follow him out of the room to let the two hackers work privately and told Jason to join him after fetching the electronic equipment from the car.

Then he summoned his wife and told her to, please, bring some tea to the fellows working in the basement and then said to Vince.

"Now let's have another drink and hear Mr. Batagliari story."

The Senator remained silent while listening to Vincenso. Only at the end he asked, "Did someone read you your rights and have you sign consent for whatever procedure they did on you?"

"I was unconscious, sir. Besides, I was a few months short of my 18th birthday, and my father had the power to sign for me. He was a high-ranking officer of the United States military. Unfortunately, they shipped me overseas after my discharge from the hospital, and Dad died before I came back, so I could never ask him what was done to me. I have tried to track down the doctors, but they refuse to talk to me. They sent me to other doctors who give me pills for PTSD. I know sir that I do not have Post Traumatic Stress Disorder, even though I do not have very pleasant memories of what we did in Afghanistan"

The Senator remained silent for a long time, then asked: "What year did you say this happened to you?"

"Two thousand and two, sir."

"Two thousand and two are you sure about that?"

"Very sure, sir. I am."

By then Jason had returned with the electronic equipment that the Patels had requested to be fetched from the car. The senator instructed him to go out again and invite House Representative Maria de La Cruz Cortez and Senator William Shuster to come to his home as soon as possible.

When Edith McClain heard the names she said, "Are you sure you want to call those two people over? They are from the opposition party. You and they have never seen eye to eye?"

42

Chapter 6
THE DOCTOR

"This is not the time for petty politics Edith, this is a truly National Emergency and it is precisely the opposite party people the ones I need. People from our party would likely align with the president, call this a hoax, and drag their feet on forever"

He scribbled two short messages and gave them to Jason: "Go, my friend. Take the same precautions because, most likely, the homes of those two will be under surveillance as well."

Jason left and the senator left Kelly and Vince in the foyer and went to his bedroom to make a private phone call.

When the person in the other end of the line answered he said, "Is this Doctor Joe Thurston?"

"Yes, it is who is calling."

"This is Jim McClain, Joe. How are you and the family?"

"They are fine, Jim. At least the ex and the two kids were fine the last time I talked with them. I do not know if you remember that I got into a nasty divorce, and not only did she take most of my money, but she turned our two grown kids against me. However, all that is in the past, and we haven't seen each other in so long. So, your call is a pleasant surprise; I haven't seen you since the Christmas party at the White House two years ago. Is everything okay with you?"

"Well, you know how it is. There are always problems in this profession. In fact, I am calling you now to ask you a question. Do you remember 'Project Enhancement.' We approved big bucks to finance it, but then we had to stop it. Do you remember what year we stopped it"

"It was the year two thousand. We stopped it because we had some serious complications."

"I remember about those complications, and that was why my committee stopped the project, but do you know if someone else did not and continue doing it after the year 2000?"

There was silence at the other end of the line, and then Dr. Thurston said, "Do not quote me on this, Jim, because there are only rumors. Apparently Bruce Colton and Neil Pratt—remember those two doctors who worked with us back then? Well, supposedly they did work in a few more subjects on the side later on, either for the military or for civilian contractors. Perhaps they did only a couple of more subjects; apparently with not-so-good results. There was an explosion in their lab and both died, actually three people died but the third body was never identified."

"Joe, this is most important and urgent, I know you have files with the names of those subjects who volunteered to participate in the project and hopefully also their current whereabouts. Can you please e-mail those files to my personal computer at home, as soon as possible."

After getting a positive response from Doctor Joe Thurston, the Senator returned downstairs to join his guest in the foyer and check on the Patel hackers, who initially gave him good news. They have been able to hack into Kelly Carter computers, both the desktop and the laptop, and were retrieving data in their flash drives.

Suddenly they stopped and said, "Fuck...it seems like they detected us!"

"Babar, remove the flash. Quickly see what we have." Then their screens went blank

Meanwhile, panic followed by confusion at the Oval Office when Kelly's computers came alive. The three men there did not know what to do.

The first to react was the General, who yanked the desktop computer from the wall outlet and then smashed it against the floor with enough force to shatter it into pieces.

Meanwhile, the vice president was trying his best to turn off the laptop without success. "This fucken thing works with batteries, and you may need a password to turn them off."

The general again grabbed the laptop from the vice president's hands and, throwing it on a couch, pulled his gun and shot six rounds into the machine, which started sputtering, producing smoke and eventually went silent.

Needless to say, than in less than thirty seconds there was a score of G-Men guns drawn bursting into the Oval Office and almost shooting the general, who still held the smoking gun in his hands.

"I am sorry, gentlemen, there was a small accident here. General Masters heard that computer making noises, and he thought we were being spied upon, so he reacted in a military way," said the president. He continued addressing the men: "Thank you men, go back to your posts, and once again thank you for the promptitude that you displayed in coming to my aid…thank you"

"Do you want us to remove the remains of those computers, sir? I do not think they will ever work again," asked one of the Secret Service agents.

"No need, Joe, thank you. The general will take them to Army Intelligence to review them, just in case. Thanks again."

Upon leaving the room, the agent named Joe said to a colleague, "That is one of the most blatant pieces of bullshit that has ever come from the mouth of this president. And by golly that he has spilled a lot of bull over the years."

Chapter 7
HELP

The Patel cousins were scared at first and then frustrated. It was clear to them that no one was working on Kelly's computers, trying to track down the hackers. It was obvious to them that the devices had been disabled or destroyed. That was reassuring as they little by little realized they had submerged themselves in a situation that was way beyond their imaginations and extremely dangerous. They were smart enough to understand that at least two men had been assassinated over the content of those computers.

They expressed their fears to Vincent and the senator—who was still anonymous to them—and who, as a small consolation, promised them ten thousand dollars each for their efforts and silence.

In the end, they accepted the money (to be delivered by Jason the next morning to their Internet café). Though they were still afraid, they offered further assistance free of charge, should their services be required in the future. After all, they said that India and Pakistan, with a population of over a billion, was likely to suffer tremendous losses if the lethal virus was ever released in their country and that the United States of America was also their country now.

Unfortunately, the information they obtained from Kelly's computers was not enough to prove their case against the president of the United States. However, there was something very useful; the features of most of the people who attended the meeting at the Oval Office could be seen clearly, especially after some enhancements made by the Patels.

When the senator viewed the tape, he was totally flabbergasted. "My God, he said that is General Masters, a real son of a bitch, ruthless and ambitious. I am not surprised to see him there. The other guy in uniform is—or was—General Colton. He is the one who was killed in the accident

46

right after leaving this meeting. The others, other than the President and vice-president, I do not know. They must be the CEOs of the drug companies Kelly mentioned. The oriental-looking guy and the well-dressed woman must be the scientists that Mrs. Carter was talking about."

"At least now, do we know exactly who we are dealing with?"

"Yes, sir, but the problem is how to deal with them," said Vince

"Well Lieutenant, we do it first through politics, and after that, or I rather say at the same time we may have to get our hands dirty."

"Do you mean to take those guys down, including the president and the vice? I am willing to try to do it."

"That won't be wise, lieutenant. An assassinated president always becomes a hero in the eyes of the people, and being a hero is the last thing this guy deserves. I wonder what has taken Jason so long to come back; I hope he did not have trouble or that my guest declined to join us."

As the senator spoke, the doorbell rang.

"That could be him. I'll take it," said the senator's wife.

"Wait a minute, Edith. Why would Jason ring the bell? Not only does he have a key to the house, but he knows that the guests tonight should come through the garage door. Let me see who it is."

The senator went to the door and put his eye to the peephole, immediately recognizing the unexpected visitor. "Guess what Edith? It is no one else than our friend Professor Joe Thurston."

Opening the door, he let in his friend, who was carrying a heavy box.

"Please come in, Joe; let me help you with that box. Surely you remember my wife, Edith. These are Mrs. Kelly Carter, whom I am sure you are familiar with, and Lieutenant Vincenso Batagliari, one of the unlisted subjects of the project that I hope you are bringing us information about."

Doctor Thurston, after shaking hands with everybody, sat down on the couch, took a sip of a drink that Mrs. McCall had poured for him and said, "Indeed, his name is not in my files. Must be one of the later ones that Colton and Pratt worked on out of the box after my time."

"Please, Joe, tell us a little about the project and what happened to it."

"Well, you may remember that I, with the assistance of my colleagues, Drs Bruce Colton and Neil Pratt, worked on a chemical—a serum—that, when injected into living subjects, enhanced their physical and mental abilities. We started working on that in the eighties. We tried it on chimps, but abandoned it because they became too strong, too clever, and so aggressive that we had to euthanize them.

Some years later, somehow, the military found out about our experiments and became very interested in them, making Congress authorize funds to continue our research. Being on the Armed Forces Committee, Jim had to supervise us, ensuring we were not wasting taxpayers' money unnecessarily.

"I personally believe—unfortunately without proof of it—that it was either Bruce or Neil who went to the military back then, asking them to fund the project," interrupted Senator McClain.

"I do to, Jim, I do too. But, unfortunately, the military is not known to be patient. So they pressured us to start trials on humans after we modified the serum to make it less strong and less likely to cause uncontrollable rage in the subjects. Then we started recruiting volunteers. We were supposed to start with six men and six women. We interviewed lots of enlisted men and made a choice among the best and fittest, and they were fully informed of their rights and possible side effects. The enrolment was totally free and voluntary."

Vince interrupted: "I certainly do not remember going through any of that."

"That is, Lieutenant, because you were not in that group. The project was terminated by Jim and his congressional committee two years before the time we think you may have been treated with the serum—or a new version of it," said Doctor Thurston.

"So, what happens next?"

"Of the twelve volunteers, only four women were treated; two women and one man died from a reaction to the serum. That was the end of it…. Congress stopped the funding, and we departed ways with Colton and Pratt. I heard nothing from them until I learned that they had died in a fire and explosion at their lab. I do not know what they were working on when that occurred."

"Whatever happened to the surviving volunteers from your experiment, Doctor?" asked Vince.

"That is what is in the files in the box. Oddly enough, the two women did exceedingly well. One is married, has two kids, is a paramedic, and, on top of that, owns—together with her husband—a dance and martial arts school. Believe it or not, the other one stayed in the army and is now a three-star general."

"And the men?" entreated Vincent.

"I am afraid, son, that the men did not do as well. Two committed suicides; three are in jail for aggravated assault, and one is a drug addict who has been in and out of jail on different charges. The last I heard of him was that he was living in the streets somewhere in Florida. We still try to keep track of them but that is not always easy."

"Well, Doctor, you can now track your seventh man as a homeless veteran living in the streets of Washington DC. And you can add that he was not a volunteer but a victim of some twisted father's pride. Do you know if there is an antidote for that serum?" said Vince.

"I am afraid there isn't one son; we have tried several medications with only limited success. The main problem is that these men are not patient and have a very short fuse. It is very hard to work with them. They expect results within days, and those medications may take weeks or months to work. So if they don't feel better in a few days, they curse you, break something, and walk away."

Vince thought that it all sounded very familiar, and although disappointed at the fact that there seemed to be no cure, at least now he knew almost certainly what had caused his problems all these years.

Chapter 8
PLAN OF ACTION

Doctor Thurston continued, "Now that I have given you the information you requested, can you tell me what is going on in here, Jim? I see that Mrs. Kelly Carter, who has officially gone nuts and is being wanted by the government, and who, as of yesterday, was playing in the opposite team is being sheltered in your home along with Lieutenant Vincenso Batagliari, who has been as well the unwilling victim of an experiment that I abandoned many years ago."

Senator James McClain responded: "Joe, this is such a serious and very, very dangerous problem that I am beginning to believe the more people are aware of it, the more secure we are; however, I do not wish to compromise your security, Joe. So, if you prefer not to be privy to what is going on, I will gladly respect that."

"Come on, Jim. We were in the war, and I am too old to be afraid. Besides, if I can be of any assistance, you can count on me. Please tell me," said the doctor.

"Okay, I'll let Mrs. Carter tell you the story and show you some pictures. Then, I'll comment and accept suggestions from any of you."

Kelly Carter told the story that, to her, felt like for the thousand times this day. When she finished, she played the flash drive on the computer.

"That is all we have, and only after some friends hacked more info from Kelly's computers. Do you, Joe, recognize some of the attendants, besides the obvious ones and the two that are no longer in this world."

"Well, I do know the Chinese guy, he is a brilliant scientist from the University of Peking who has been doing some research here at Harvard for the last couple of years, I believe his name is Chin Gan do, and the woman is as bright as he is, and also works at Harvard; her name is Lidia

Deltoro, and I think she is half-Mexican. Did not know they were working together."

"Anyone else?" asked the Senator

"I do recognize some of the guys from big pharma, but I do not know their names or backgrounds. I do know General John Masters, a real son of a bitch. If you ask me, a true psychopath. I bet that, right now, he is putting together a team of men like him to track Mrs. Carter down, along with whoever else is helping her."

"Oh my God!" cried Kelly. "And only Jason and Vince among us can even use a weapon. We are as good as dead."

"No we aren't, not only the Senator and I can also use a weapon, but we can assemble a team as good, or better than the one Masters can put together," said Doctor Thurston.

"And where are we going to find those men?" asked Vincent.

"Right here, my friend, right here," said the doctor, patting on the boxes with the files of the individuals who had received the serum. "We start with the General; her name is Silvia Fuentes. I am certain that she be willing to help stop this madness. They should help us, first, to secure Doctor Lidia and Doctor Go, and then find and destroy the virus."

"Great idea, and at the same time, Kelly and I will work on destroying the president," said Senator McClain and then asked Vince, "Would you mind telling the Patels if they can be nice enough to record on a disk or flash drive, Mrs. Carter's story. I'm sure she is tired of repeating it so frequently. So if we can record it, she won't have to keep repeating it. "Would you mind doing it, Mrs. Carter?"

"Of course not, Senator. I'll be more than glad, especially since it would spare me from telling the story over and over again," said Kelly Carter.

As soon as Vince returned from talking to the Patels in the basement, he signaled Kelly to follow him downstairs.

Doctor Joe Thurston and Senator James McClain were alone in the library. Edith McClain brought a pot of coffee and several cups saying to the men, "I think is going to be a long night, you men better get ready for it."

"Where did you park your car, Joe?" asked the Senator.

"No car, tonight I took an Uber to come here. It dropped me off about half a block from this house, and I did not start walking until he disappeared. I guess I am not as young and strong as I used to be. I had to stop and rest several times; that box is heavy."

"That was wise but probably unnecessary, Joe, because we have two spooks in a car across the street watching my house. Likely they took your picture and by now they are running it in some computer, who knows where."

"Irrelevant, my dear James. I have government clearance and I am sure that they are aware that you and I been friends for long time we have been. My field of expertise is not virology, and, as far as I know, they do not know that you are sheltering Kelly Carter in your house."

"You are correct, Joe. Now we need to decide how to proceed next. I am expecting a couple of other guests, and I would appreciate it if you could stay to meet them, in case you have not done so before. Let us drink some coffee because my dear Edith is right. This is going to be a very long night. Just pray that we see the morning."

"Then, as soon as your guests leave, we should go to see General Fuentes. Thank God I have her private cell phone number . . . you see, I still try to keep tabs on all my old subjects. Perhaps it is due to my conscience bothering me. I consider General Silvia a good friend, more than a patient."

"When are your guests supposed to arrive?"

"They should be here by now; if they agree to come, Jason is bringing them. He is very persuasive, but I am afraid that he is taking too long. Edith, has Jason contacted you? I am beginning to worry."

No sooner than the senator finished the phrase that they heard the garage door open and a car pulling into it

It was Jason.

Chapter 9
JASON

Every time Jason White walked into a room, he attracted the eyes of everyone in it; he was over six feet tall, and his eyes were hazel, which was unusual on a black man. His head was shaved to a shine, as was his face. However, rough in certain ways, it was not threatening but attractive. He dressed impeccably, always wearing a suit, black, blue, or gray, a white shirt, and a single-color tie. He wore a bulletproof vest under the shirt, and it made him look more muscular; Jason always carried a 9mm Smith & Wesson in a holster under his arm and a Ruger LCP 380 strapped to his left ankle, plus a bowie knife strapped to his right ankle.

Jason was an ex-marine and ex-CIA agent, having been fired by the agency after a mission failed—through no fault of his. He was not in charge, not the leader of the mission, but he was the only black guy left alive in the team (two others were killed) and thus became the fall guy. It cost him his pension and his family, as his wife divorced him and took full custody of his twins (boy and girl), who were currently attending school somewhere in France.

Senator McClain was already on the Armed Forces Committee and was privy to the information about this man, being able to see that he had been unjustly and unfairly treated and called to offer him a job as his bodyguard and driver. Ever since, they became more than friends—they had become family, to the point that he had his own room at McClain's home and spent more time there than he did in his own duplex. Jason White will willingly and gladly give his life for the Senator and his wife.

So, Jason, that night, walked with the man and a woman who had come with him into the library of Senator James McClain's home.

The woman was younger and prettier than a US

congresswoman is pictured to be, and the man who came with her was older and distinguishes looking, fitting the picture of a US senator.

Senator McClain got up from his chair to greet the newcomers: "Representative Cortez, Senator Shuster, welcome. I am honored to receive you in my house, and I apologize for the inconvenience of this unusual call. May I introduce you to my friend Doctor Joe Thurston and offer you a drink?"

"Scotch, whiskey, wine, coffee, soda, brandy. We even have water if you prefer."

Nobody laughed at the intended joke, so after clearing his throat, McClain introduced Doctor Thurston to them. Edith brought red zinfandel for the woman and poured a half glass of Scotch to Shuster.

"I trust that my good friend Jason treated you well."

"Well, he is polite but intimidating. One is almost afraid of saying no to him," said Maria Cortez.

"Is that so, Senator? Then, allow me to apologize for him."

"Also, he brought us here in a stolen vehicle," she continued.

The senator was amused but pretended to be upset. "Is that true, Jason? How did that happen? You left here in your car."

"Well, boss, this is what happened. I figured that I needed a vehicle that the spooks would not recognize and one that was easy to get in and out without being seen, such as a van with sliding doors in the sides. It was too late to rent one, so I figured I would borrow one. I drove to the long-term airport parking, left my car there, and looked for the kind of car I needed. I made sure the tires and engine were still warm, indicating the owner would be gone for a while. I left my car at the airport and drove to the senator's home, leaving the vehicle about a block away, knowing their doors and giving them your message and your note, plus a brief briefing. At first, they hesitated but then they became curious and agreed to come. So I walked back to the vehicle, stopped in front of their door, opened the van's side door, and let them slide inside. The same scenario was repeated at both places, I picked Senator Shuster first because I figured the congresswoman would be trustier and more confident if she saw a familiar face with me. Don't worry, boss, I shall return that vehicle to the airport tonight."

"That was extremely clever, Jason, but also a bit reckless. I trust nothing will happen to that car. Now, if you allow me, let's go to the reason I invited you here tonight. First, let me warn you that this is something extremely dangerous and a prime national security issue. Lives have already been lost. So, if you decline to participate, I will respect your decision but you be compelled to keep absolute secrecy, whether you be in or out."

Senator Shuster said, "First, we need to know what this is all about, and yes, I swear to keep whatever it is secret. Yet, if it is a matter of national security, I am a sworn server of this country and willing to defend it, no matter what."

"Likewise," said the woman.

"Very well, then. Can you, Jason, please go into the basement and invite the Lieutenant and the Lady to come up and join us. Also see if our other friends have finished with making the recordings I asked them to make, and if so, please drive them back home, perhaps in the car you borrowed so you can return it as well"

"Yes, Senator, I am on it."

A few minutes later, he returned with Kelly and Vince. "Our other friends said they are done, sir. Here are the recordings. I will be back as soon as possible."

The visiting senators could not hide their surprise at recognizing Kelly, who, according to the news, was supposed to have gone crazy and taken off to who knows where.

They shook hands and the senator introduced Vince, without telling them anything about his problematic story. "Mrs. Carter is why I invited you to my home with such secrecy and urgency, but you will see, after listening to her, that we have a serious national security problem on our hands, and we need to work together on that. I am aware that

Mrs. Carter is probably more than tired of telling her story over and over, so I have some friends make a recording of it, however, if she prefers to tell it one more time, I will not have any objection."

"I know Senator Cortez and Senator Shuster, and although we have worked on opposite political sides, I believe that they are honest and patriotic people. I certainly would not mind telling the story one more time to them"

Kelly Carter told her story to Senator Shuster and US Representative Maria de La Cruz Cortez.

Chapter 10
LEOPOLD

The man was sitting alone at the end of the bar. There were only a few patrons, as it was a weekday and past 10 p.m. He was drinking vodka on ice and pretending to pay attention to the soccer game on the TV above the bar.

His name was Leopold. Leopold Mishanivich and he was born in Russia.

Leopold was a tall man, probably in his late forties, with chopped salt and pepper hair and a mustache and beard matching his hair color. Their eyes were gray and cruel, but what made him stand out was the large scar from his left ear down to his chin, barely disguised by the beard.

The establishment door opened, and a man wearing a black trench coat and dark shades walked in. Upon seeing the newcomer, the man at the end of the bar finished his drink in one gulp but did not get up until after the man who had just arrived approached him and said very close to his ear: "If you are Leopold. The general is waiting for you in his car. Please follow me."

Leopold put twenty dollars on the counter and followed the other guy without waiting for his tab.

The bartender did not argue.

Leopold followed the man around the corner where a black Chevy Blazer SUV with the windows tinted so dark, nobody could see inside even if the inside lights were on.

The driver came out and asked Leopold if he was armed. He did not respond, but by his attitude it was evident that he was carrying and also that he did not let anyone to frisk him or take his weapon.

A voice came from inside the car: "It's okay, guys, let him be. He is a friend. Come in, Leopold."

It was General Charles Flynn Masters

"Strange to get a call from you, General. I have not heard

from you since you got me out of the cold, at the end of the Cold War and sent me to El Salvador to clean the dirt you guys left in there."

The General did not respond, only saying: "Hello, Leopold. You look well, other than that scar on your face."

Leopold did not like that remark, as he was very sensitive about his appearance and very conscious about the scar. Still, he chose to ignore the remark and just responded, "Sometimes you have to pay the price for doing other people's dirty work or fighting other people's wars"

"Yeah! I heard that. You have been doing well, doing a lot of mercenary work and some other not-too-legal business on the side here and there. That is why I would like to hire you and your team. I have a job for you to do; a job that, so far seems rather easy, and we are willing to pay you handsomely for it."

"I am listening, General, but before, I like to know how handsome is handsome. I do not work for cheap and if the job requires to involve more men, the price goes up."

General Masters was not known to be the most generous person, even when not spending his own money, so he said, "Ten thousand now and ten thousand more after it is done."

Leopold laughed, "That is what any mobster or cartel would pay for whacking off a street vendor. If a high-rank general with thousands of men under his command comes to Leopold for help, the job must be serious and dirty."

"Okay . . . I am willing to double that, but I want to be done as fast as possible."

"No deal, General. Multiply it by five and I would consider it."

The general was livid because, while the President had put at his disposition $250,000, he had been planning to keep most of it for himself. Finally he agreed to pay Leopold fifty thousand now and the other fifty when he finished the mission. After that, perhaps he could be able to get rid of Leopold for good and keep the total $250,00. So he said, "Okay, $100,000 with fifty now and another fifty at the end of the job."

The general had anticipated this bargaining, so he opened his brief case a showed stacks of bills amounting to $100,000, counted half of it, and gave it to Leopold, who said, "I do not have anything to carry this money with me. So, I will take the briefcase as a souvenir, and you keep the loose bills. Now, what is it that you want me to do, General?"

The general pulled out a picture of Kelly Carter from the inner pocket of his coat and another picture of Kelly's friend Laura. He showed both to Leopold. "I want you to locate these women, take them to a secure location, and call me. I need to know how much they know and who they have contacted. After that, make them disappear forever.

"You may start by visiting the other woman. Her name is Laura Mason, and she is the last person our person of interest contacted by Kelly."

"Oh...I see. This is the woman who went nuts at the White House this morning. I assume she is not nuts and knows something compromising to you." And Leopold continued. "This seems big. Maybe I should have asked you for more money . . . but I am a man of his word. Besides, I owe you. Obviously, you like to interrogate the Carter woman once we capture her?"

"That would be the idea. But I would prefer if I can do that in private. It sounds risky, yet . . . yes, I do. I want to be the one asking her questions. Call me on this cell phone when you have her, and I will call you as soon as we know who is helping her. Because we are sure that someone is helping her, not sure yet who, or if it is more than one person. But I want them put out of the picture for good as well. So, best put together a team. Not too many, probably three or four men will do.

"Oh, Leo, one more thing. After taking care of the women, I want you to go fetch these other two people. One is a Chinese doctor, and the other is a Mexican-American doctor. There is no need for violence here. Just make sure they do not see the women and the women don't see them. Call me as soon as you have them with the cell I gave you. Here are the addresses of all four of them. You have until before sunrise to report to me. It's best to memorize the addresses and destroy the paper afterward."

"Okay, General, you will hear from me soon."

"I hope so, Leopold."

Leopold was a Russian-born but British-educated man who had worked for the KGB for several years. When the Russians invaded Afghanistan, he was sent there to perform covert operations. This did not include getting involved in the poppy and drug derivatives trade, not less without the Russian government's knowledge. Unfortunately for him, the Russians found out about his collateral business, and he was about to be captured and sent back to the Soviet Union and then, probably to Siberia.

So, Leopold decided to escape the Soviets and surrender to the Americans who were running covert operations for the benefit of the Taliban, which was fighting the Russians. Therefore, Leopold was picked up by a small group of Americans commanded by the then Captain Charles Flynn Masters and eventually given asylum in the US.

This was due mainly to the fact that Leopold, being then more of a con man than a warrior, duped Masters into believing that he had a wealth of secret information to pass on to the Americans and was willing to provide it free of charge, but of course, not before he was given asylum in the USA.

Masters, being ambitious and hoping that bringing such a valuable asset would foster his career, believed Leopold's story and sponsored him in obtaining US citizenship.

By the time the CIA came to realize that Leopold was just a minor player, it was too late and too embarrassing to reverse course. So they let him stay in the US and used him from time to time to take part in small operations in Central and South America, primarily dealings related with the Colombian and Mexican drug cartels.

However, Leopold could not help himself by staying out of trouble. So once again, within a couple of years, he was helping the Cartels in bringing drugs into the US. This time, he was not that lucky, as the CIA tipped the DEA about Leopold's drug activities. He was captured and sent to federal prison for ten years.

However, Leopold's luck had not completely abandoned him. Two years into his imprisonment, he got word that some doctors were recruiting volunteers among inmates for some experiment with a new drug. He and his cellmate volunteered in exchange for a reduction of sentence to five years.

Unfortunately, something went wrong, and those doctors, plus the volunteer who was his cellmate, perished in a fire that started in their laboratory. Leopold was severely burned, mostly over his back and buttocks. At the same time, a piece of broken, hot glass flew and lodged into the side of his face. The event lead to several weeks in the hospital and plastic surgery that only partially helped, as he was left with a seriously scared back and an ugly scar on his face.

Leopold never knew for sure if it was because of that ordeal or because of the serum that the Doctors were injecting him, but after that, he became a totally different kind of man. He did not remember much about the experiment, or the Doctor. He knew he had to sign a paper consenting to participate and he remembered that his friend and cellmate went for two or three days to "get the treatment", which apparently had to be administered over several days. Leopold remembered only going once, for the first time, after days of getting blood test, scans, X-rays etc. On that fateful day, he went into the lab, was put on a gurney inside of a glass cubicle. Someone inserted a needle in his vein. He remembered hearing some discussion, some shouting, sounds of things being broken, and—he believed it was his friend causing that commotion—then the fire started, and everything went blank.

After that, Leopold became a soldier of fortune, at times helping the CIA in some dirty operations, other times shipping weapons to rebels in Africa, the Middle East, or the Colombian and Mexican drug cartels, as well as doing some drug smuggling himself. From a likable, mostly inoffensive con man, Leopold Mishanivich transformed into a cruel, ruthless man who did not have any problem killing, torturing, or raping without regard for cause, religion, sex, or race. He became stronger, ruthless, and fearless. Or at the very least, less cowardly than he had been,

He suspected that this change was due to the serum that those American doctors injected into him while he was taken out of prison.

Chapter 11
THE CONGRESSPERSONS

Senator McClain was addressing the guests at his mansion, first directing his words to the congresspersons before addressing the other people present:

"Please listen to me first and then you are free to state your opinions and stance."

"As I said before, my fellow congresspersons, I have invited you to my home tonight because, although we are not in the same side of the aisle, and we are not friends, we know each other and I hope that you have formed an opinion of me, as I have of each of you."

"You should know that I am human and therefore not perfect, but you also should know me as a patriot and as someone who sides with the side of reason and justice. I believe you are like that as well, and that your patriotism, loyalty and honesty would prevail over your political convictions and cheap party loyalties.

"There has not been a situation like this perhaps in the whole history of our country; we have had presidents that have been cheaters, liars, womanizers, even thieves. We have had some that have led us to unjustified wars either for pride, profit, or error. But we never had a fellow that is willing negotiate with a potential foe of our democracy and willing to kill thousands—perhaps millions of people—simply for profit. Even Hitler, in his feeble mind, believed he did the horrendous things he did for the good of the German people."

The senator stopped there to catch his breath, suddenly realizing that he was not in a political rally but addressing fellow congresspersons in his own house. So he took a sip of his brandy, apologized to his listeners, who were actually mesmerized by his speech, and continued in less dramatic terms.

"Sorry, I know you have listened to Mrs. Carter and heard

the recording, therefore it is obvious that we have to stop this mad man from carrying out his plans, remove him from office, and send him to prison. Lieutenant Batagliari here wants to kill him—and of course he deserves that—but that would also make him a martyr, a hero and nobody will believe our history. No, we should attack him from several fronts at least. First the political, then the economic, and third by preventing such a lethal virus from being released on the population"

"Congresswoman Cortez, Senator Shuster and I would be in charge of the first front. Doctor Thurston, Lieutenant Batagliari, Jason and I would take on the second front. However, I am not going to force you to do anything. This is probably going to be more dangerous than we can imagine and most likely our lives would be endangered. So, please consider seriously your participation before you give agree or disagree. If you have questions, please ask now."

"I do not have questions, and I am in," said Congress-woman Cortez.

"Neither do I," said Senator Shuster "Just figure how to proceed."

"I leave it up to you," said Senator McClain, "but I personally believe that you should make privy of this information as many people as you can trust."

"Senator McClain is right," said Maria Cortez and continued. "I believe we have first disclosed this information only to those colleagues that we know and trust and then ask them to do likewise. Moreover, I believe we should only play to them the tape, drive—whatever—where Kelly Carter is telling her story. Although we can confirm that there is recording of the White House meeting, we only should tell them that several copies have been made of it and all are in safe places. We should not let them listen to it because what was recorded is not that much compromising and they may be reluctant to believe the whole story."

"Good point," said McClain, "but of course both of you shall be provided with copies of that flash drive to be used at your discretion. And I cannot emphasize enough the great danger to the lives of those of us who are, or will be, in possession of such drive.

"That is one more reason why we should start calling people as soon as possible—even tonight—as this is a national emergency," said Bill Shuster. "And, if you think about it, if the president's men become aware that members of congress have been privy of his plot, he will hesitate to carry on his nefarious plans. After all, he will not dare to kill all the members of congress"

Vince Battaglia spoke for the first time—and out of turn: "Unless you all are together in one place and, BOOM, a bomb blows you all into bits."

Shuster replied, "I do not think he will dare, but just in case we shall meet in small groups"

"We will start this very same night then," said Congresswoman Maria Cortez. "Is there anything else you want to tell us, Senator McClain? If not, you may add to your qualifications that you have big cojones. Good night, you all. Hope to see you soon, all in one piece."

"Do you think your friend Jason has left with the car he borrowed? It is less likely that whoever is watching this house will see us in it," said Senator Shuster.

"I believe he left to take home our friend the hackers, but I could take you in my car," said Senator McClain.

As they were speaking, they heard the garage door and Mrs. McClain said, "I believe Jason is back. Not sure what car he is driving, but he seems to have arrived."

Seconds later Jason walked into the room, his imposing physique casting a shadow before him and said, "The hackers have been delivered, boss. However, I kept the van for a bit longer 'cause I figured you would order me to take the lady representative and the senator back to their homes".

Senator McClain just sighed and said to Jason, "Just make sure you deliver them before the owner of that vehicle reports it stolen. It would be extremely embarrassing and most detrimental to the job ahead if you are arrested and charged with car theft."

"If that happens, sir, they can tell the cops that I kidnapped them. Ready when you are, lady and gentleman."

At his remark from Jason, everyone laughed and got up ready to leave.

"One last question," said the Senator. "Does any of you own a gun. I know both of you are for gun control?"

Maria Cortez answered, "We are not against citizens owning a firearm. We are for some form of control and regulation and for the banning of assault type rifles. But responding to your question, Senator, yes, I own a pistol and a shotgun, and know how to use them, too."

Senator William Shuster answered in similar terms. "I have the same idea about firearms as Representative Cortez. I served in Kuwait with the reserves and also own an AR-15 for defense and practice."

"Did not mean to offend either one of you or I am reassured by your response, just let me suggest that you keep your weapons not too far from you after tonight," said Senator McClain.

Chapter 12
THE GENERAL

After the congresspersons left, the senator, Vince Batagliari, Kelly Carter, Doctor Joe Thurston, and Mrs. McClain were left in the room. The senator spoke to his wife, "Dear, why don't you take Mrs. Carter upstairs to her room. She must be terribly tired, as she had a very hectic day. Joe, the Lieutenant and I have yet something else to do."

Reluctantly, Kelly agreed to follow Edith McClain, because she really was very tired. Yet she knew that it was going to be hard for her to go to sleep, in spite of the "sleepy time" tea that the lady of the house brought to her room.

"If you gentleman excuse me, I am going to make a phone call," said Dr. Thurston

"Who you are calling, Joe?" asked McClain

"A three-star General Silvia Fuentes-Graham," was the answer

"Good thinking; but wasn't she one of your subjects? And is she still at PSD?"

"Yes, to your first question Jim, and to the second, I believe she is, but she does not live there. She has an apartment in town."

"PSD, isn't that the mental disease that some doctor said I have?" intervened Vince.

"Close, but that is PTSD, Post Traumatic Stress Disorder: a condition quite common among soldiers who have been in combat. Now, in the military it stands for Personal Security Detail," Dr Thurston clarified. "They are, I believe, part of the Marine Corps. And, no, you do not have it, unless it is on top of the effects of the serum, they injected you with. However, I doubt very much that you have PTSD, Lieutenant," corrected Dr. Thurston.

Someone picked up the line and Dr. Thurston exchanged a few words with the person on the other end and said, "We are in. Silvia, will be expecting us at her apartment. Batagliari, you be the designated driver. Jim, you are coming, of course. A US senator with your reputation will enforce our credibility with the general. She is extremely smart and can almost read what is in our heads".

"I see your point, Joe. However, I am handling the political side of this problem and before this night is done, I need to talk to as many of my colleagues as possible. So I will go just be for a brief introduction and then leave. I have to go see a lot of people," said Senator McClain.

"Fair enough, Jim. We can call an Uber to get back or go wherever, and you take the car," said the doctor

"Doctor, you mentioned that this general is not only a she, but also was injected with the same shit that they injected me. How in the world did she become a general if she had to face the same problems that I have?" asked Vincent as they were walking the garage.

"That will require some more detailed explanation, which I believe you deserve, and which I will gladly provide you with later. Suffice to say that the serum worked much differently in women than in men. Either killed them or made them superwomen. Now you have to concentrate on driving."

"We are being tailed, gentlemen."

"Hopefully you can be able to shake our tail without killing us in the process."

As Jason's van and the senator's car left the garage almost at the same time, the Secret Service guys were confused as to which to follow. After a few seconds of hesitation, it seemed more logical to follow the senator's car, which they did.

Senator McClain's mansion was located on what was known as "Embassy Row", between Connecticut and Massachusetts Avenues, east of Rock Creek. General Fuentes apartment was located near Tyler Park, at the other side of the river, close to Highway 66. That was, logically, the best way to get there. However, there was the problem of shaking their tail. As the traffic was light at that hour, Vince drove first at normal speed, taking smaller roads and then, as a traffic light changed from green to yellow, he sped up, letting the car behind stop at a red light. Then, after making sure that they were no longer being followed, took Route 66 near the airport.

They arrived at the General's apartment building in less than 20 minutes. The apartment building was four stories high, nice but not elegant, and there was no night watch or doormen. However, there was an elevator, and the lobby was deserted.

The men got into the elevator and pushed the button for the third floor and then look for apartment 333.

General Silvia Fuentes-Graham opened the door herself. She was dressed casually in jeans and a loose T-shirt that revealed she was not wearing a bra. She appeared to be in her early forties but was probably older than that, considering her military rank. She was about 5 feet, 10 inches tall, had raven-black hair that she wore long, just below the level of her shoulders. Her eyes were turquoise green and she was wearing only enough makeup to make her lips gloss pink and her cheeks rosy. She was barefooted.

The woman was wonderful overall, but it was obvious that she was not expecting to receive visitors other than Professor Dr. Thurston, with whom she seemed quite familiar. She, therefore, was surprised and a bit embarrassed when Thurston introduced his companions, especially the senator; however, she quickly regained her composure and asked them to come in.

A big German shepherd dog entered, barking in a menacing way and standing behind her. It sat still and quiet at her command without leaving her side.

"Silvia, I am sure you have met Senator James McClain, and this is Lieutenant Vincenso Batagliari; he has been a 'subject'—like you—except he was not a voluntary one. But we can talk about that later. We are not here concerning that."

And then, introducing her to his companions, Dr. Thurston said, "Gentlemen, this is General Silvia Fuentes-Graham, an old friend and an early subject of my experiments with the enhancing serum. A very successful subject, if I can add that and hope you do not mind mentioning that, because

69

these gentlemen have had access to my old files and have sworn absolute secrecy about the matter."

Silvia responded, addressing him as Professor, "As long as you trust them and there is secrecy, I would not object."

As the dog was still growling and staying by her, she ordered him to lie down and said to her visitors, "Please don't mind Czar. He is very protective of me, but won't attack anyone unless I tell him to do so. He is a war dog and has been my buddy since Afghanistan. So, please come in and sit down. Can I offer you a drink? Wine? Beer? Whiskey? coffee?, Water?"

"Nothing for me Silvia, thank you. We had some drinks at the home of the senator and that was enough for me. Besides, I have the feeling that this is going to be a very long night. I am not sure if the senator or the lieutenant care for something," said Thurston.

Both, the Senator and Vince declined coffee or alcohol but accepted some ice water while Thurston proceeded to tell her the reason for their visit in a rather dramatic way.

"Silvia, we need your help. As a general of the United States Armed Forces, who has sworn loyalty to this country, we request your help, we need your help. Your Country, our country needs your help." He proceeded to give the story of the genocidal plan of the President, first in his own dramatic ways, then by playing the recording of the story of Kelly Carter and the recording of the conversations in the Oval Office.

To state that General Fuentes was flabbergasted after hearing it would be an understatement and her first reaction was one of disbelief. But she was convinced after hearing that two of the attendees at the Oval Office meeting had conveniently suffered accidents she was willing to help.

"How I can help"? was her question.

Professor Thurston responded, "The president must be removed from office, and also the vice-president, but not by violence because we don't want to make him a hero. There is no question about that. But it has to be done politically and Senator Jim McClain, here is already starting things in

70

preparation for an impeachment and a press release. However, being that this man has a base of totally fanatical followers—both among the people and in Congress—he can likely go on TV, deny everything, and accuse the press and us of plotting to overthrow the government. Therefore, we need proof, we need a witness, and we need to obtain a sample of the virus."

"And how you propose to do that, Professor Joe?" asked General Fuentes.

"That is what we need your help for General. We need to kidnap the Chinese scientist, Dr. Chin Ghan Do, and the woman who works with the professor, Lidia Del Toro. But we need at least half a dozen men, for which the senator has suggested recruiting the survivors of the enhancement serum experiment. So far, we only have two: you and Lieutenant Batagliari,"

"I seem to remember you saying back then that there were twelve subjects. I know about Karla Messer being alive and well, but what about the other ten? What did become of them, professor?" asked the general.

"It is a sad story, general Fuentes. We had six women and six men. We were supposed to give each three infusions of the serum, three and seven days apart. At first everything went nice and smooth. You and a man known by the code name "Moose" were the first two and both were very successful. At least, we thought so at the time. Karla was the third and also successful, but the next two women died after the third infusion. So did one of the men. Therefore, we stop the experiment."

"So you saying, professor, that you administered the serum to only three of us? And how about your lieutenant friend here? He looks younger than us. Why did you give the serum to him?"

"The answer to the first part of your question is, no, we gave the serum to ten of your fellow soldiers because those who died did so days after the treatment."

Professor Thurston paused to take a drink of water and continued.

"We learned, much later on, that although women seemed

to be more sensitive to adverse effects on a short-term basis, they do much better than men in the long run. While women, like you and Karla, are living fruitful and productive lives, the men have done pretty miserably, as my Lieutenant Friend here, can attest. He has become homeless due to the inability to function in civilian life."

"And the answer to your second question is also a no. I did not give the serum to him. Apparently after he had an accident during boot camp and lost consciousness, then his father, who was a high-ranking military chieftain, somehow knew about the serum. He requested that my, now deceased, colleagues, Dr. Neil Pratt and Dr. Christian Shaw administer it to his unconscious son, who was still few weeks under age at the time. The Lieutenant just learned some of these facts tonight".

"Then what happened to the others, Dr Thurston?"

"The two surviving women and one surviving man were honorably discharged. The other five men were returned to duty. They performed exceedingly well in combat but had episodes of uncontrollable rage and were discharged with the diagnoses of PTSD, same as the Lieutenant here. Two are in a military prison after beating up an officer. Two became drunken drug addicts and homeless. One is in jail, here in Washington. Another committed suicide. I have tried to follow and help all of them over the years, but they have a tendency to disappear.

"Also, I have been working on trying to find a medication or a combination of medications to counteract the adverse effects of the serum, while leaving the positive effects in place. At one point Pratt, Shaw and I were very close to developing something but then their lab caught fire and all their research was lost."

During all this conversation, the senator had been ready to leave, but he remained standing by the door and at this point intervened in the conversation:

"Come on, Joe. How you plan to recruit those people, especially on short notice. And, more so, how do you plan to control such unpredictable fellows?"

"Well, Jim, remember we have been with the Lieutenant here for several hours and so far, he has not attacked any of us. Also, I have noticed during all these years that I have been following them that, oddly enough, they don't show aggression towards women. All have either been divorced or left by their wives or lovers due to their behavior, mostly towards others. I think they will respect and follow orders from General Fuentes without any hesitation or trouble. But first we have to find them and set them free."

"I probably can free the guys held by the military if you give me the names," said General Fuentes.

"One is James Timberland, but he is better known as 'Moose.' The other is Kirk White, aka 'Wolf' and the other two are Richard Boone aka 'Badger,' who is in jail, and Leroy Smith aka 'Rabbit' all those were code names we gave them and somehow they stuck. Apparently they like those. Incidentally, General Fuentes, you are 'Tigress,' and Karla is 'Lioness.'"

"I think I like that code name, Professor, it kind of fits me."

"I always thought so, General, I always thought so," said Doctor Thurston.

At this Senator McClain opened the door, but before he stepped outside, he said, "By the way, I never asked Mrs. Carter how she got my home phone number, especially since she did not have her cell phone with her."

"Oh, she called a friend of hers, I believe her name is Laura, and got it from her, I did tell her that it was a mistake because they probably could trace that call"

"Shit!" exclaimed both the senator and the general at the same time.

"That person may be in danger right now. Let me call my wife for her name and address. I believe we should check on her. I was going to go make the rounds with my colleagues' senators and representatives, but this seems to be more important, and you may need my car."

"You are right, Senator, but your role in this is most important, and we do not need your car. We can use mine. Go

73

ahead and call your wife and give us the address of this Laura," said Vince.

Once the Senator got the information, General Fuentes put some sneakers and a Colt 45 on her waist. After checking the clip and grabbing a spare one, said, "Let's go check on this chick."

Chapter 13
LAURA

The man drove around the block couple of times, slowly, just a bit below the speed limit. The house was lit and he saw through one of the windows that a TV was on. So there were people in the house, but he did not yet know how many.

He drove around the block one more time and parked his car in the street behind the house. He got out of the car, put on a black skullcap and gloves and tried to see if he could make his way to the house crossing the yards of the homes behind the one he was targeting.

But he decided that was risky. So he left the car and walked around the block. He was only scouting the area in the house. He had left three of his men in another car a few blocks behind and was supposed to call them if necessary. Then luck struck, and he figured that he could do the job alone without paying the men and save more for himself.

As he was approaching the house he saw the door opening and a man and two kids about 10 and 12 came out, the man shouting, "Are you sure you do not want to go to the movies with us?" He must have received a negative answer as he said, "Okay, dear, I do not want you to be alone. I'll just drop the kids at the mall cinema and come back. We can go together to pick them up".

The husband did not see the man standing behind a tree only few yards away who now was believing that he was the luckiest man in the world, the target—his target—had been left alone in the house and he had at least forty minutes to do what he was sent to do, and perhaps have some fun at the same time. So he waited few minutes for the car to disappear behind a corner and started walking to the house.

He went into the yard at the side of the house and looked through the windows. The girl was alone. He had figured, apparently rightly so, that he did not need any help to subdue this woman, who did not look threatening at all.

Laura was a dark-haired woman in her early forties. She was sitting on a couch on front of a television set, drinking a glass of red wine and eating popcorn. Her back was turned away from the window from which he was observing her. He could tell she her legs stretched with her bare feet on top of a table, he could tell that she was pretty and well-formed, the kind of women who diets and goes to the gym; the kind of women that he liked to play with and, yes, he was going to play. He was sure the general would not mind if he had some fun while carrying the mission he was assigned to perform.

There was no need to break the window glass. She might hear that and scream or—worse—call the cops or alert the neighbors. So he went around to the back door and opened it with ease, walking into the house without a problem. He did not even bother to cover his face. After all, there would be no witness after he finished the job.

To the police, it would appear as an ordinary case of rape and robbery…with murder

Laura Mason did not hear any noise, as the man moved like a ghost behind her, and only became aware as one gloved hand closed her mouth and another gloved hand, yielding a knife came to scratch her neck.

"Do not scream Laura. Promise you won't scream, and I will take my hand off your mouth, the knife will remain in your neck in case you feel like screaming and until you answer some questions for me."

Laura assented with a moment of her head and he lifted slightly the hand that covered her mouth.

For several seconds she could not utter a sound and her eyes were so wide open that they appear that will come out of the sockets.

"What do you want? There is little money in this house, but you can take anything you want, everything. Just do not hurt me…please," said Laura.

"We will get to that, lady, but first answer a question. You received a call this morning from a friend of yours who is missing, Mrs. Kelly Carter. Do you remember that?"

Laura nodded yes. She was beginning to realize that this

was not just a robbery, that this guy was not Secret Service or FBI, and also noticed that the guy was not even bothering to cover his face despite of having a large scar that made him easy to identify. She realized with horror that this man was probably going to kill her, so her only hope was to play dumb in the hope that her husband would return sooner than expected, although that would put him at risk of being killed.

"I do not know what you are talking about, sir. I receive lots of calls every day. I happen to have many friends, some of them in high places."

"Oh, so you want to play dumb with me. That will not work. I can be very persuasive, and I get very, very angry when people treat me as if I was stupid. Let's start over. Whose phone number did Kelly Carter ask you for?" Leopold asked as he jumped over the couch and placed himself in front of her.

He lowered the knife down to her leg and made a superficial cut on the inside of her left thigh, just above her knee. Blood started oozing and she grimaced in pain.

Laura was terrified but realized that she had to do something, as this man likely was going to rape her and kill her. Mustering all the strength and valor she could, she flexed both of her legs and kicked the man in the groin. It worked...temporarily: he screamed in pain, bent over, and dropped the switchblade knife.

Laura took advantage of this by getting up, grabbing her cell phone from the table and running upstairs, hoping to get to a room, lock herself in and call the police.

Unfortunately, the Scarface man recovered fast and jumped across the table, knocking it over and spilling the wine glass and the bottle, which broke upon hitting the floor. Within seconds he was after her, grabbing her left foot and pulling her down. He pulled the seam of the nightgown she was wearing, ripping it apart and allowing her breast and all the way to her lumbar area to be exposed.

The man became immediately aroused. With an evil smile, he pulled her harder, making her head hit at least three of the steps hard. In addition, he hit her on the face twice with an open hand, and, as she continued to struggle, he did hit her with a close fist. Laura felt the taste of her own blood in her mouth and became groggy, but did not pass out until he hit her once more with a closed fist. He grabbed her cell phone, put it in one of his pockets, and proceeded to cut her nightgown and her panties.

Laura was in a daze and hoped he would kill her now rather than endure what she knew was now coming.

Then the doorbell rang, and somebody shouted, "Laura…Mrs. Mason, are you okay? Please open the door!"

Silvia, who was used to giving orders, yielded Vince and Doctor Thurston a command. "You guys check the windows and the back door….There is always a back door."

Vince went looking for a back door, while the doctor went to check the windows. He was the first one to detect an anomaly. "Something is wrong, guys. The TV is on, but nobody is watching it and the table in front of the TV is overturned."

Vince heard the Doctor, and when he found the back door open, he walked into the house with his gun in hand and strongly felt "that thing" coming over him.

Leopold knew that people were coming and that there was more than one, most likely not just a curious neighbor. He had to get out fast, but he was not going to leave any witnesses behind. He had made the mistake of thinking that this was an easy job and that he did not need to cover his features, since he was planning to kill "the target" anyway.

He thought of the man who trained him back in Russia, many years before. He always said, "There is no such thing as an easy job. Shit can always happen, and you must be prepared to wipe it fast or you will get smeared."

Leopold got up, pulled up his pants, which he had dropped, fastened his belt, and, with his free hand, stabbed Laura in the chest with the switchblade.

After putting the knife back in his pocket Leopold pulled a gun and shot twice at the chandelier in the middle of the room, succeeding in killing the lights, then sensing, more than seeing, the presence of Vincenso, coming through the kitchen, fired two more shots in that directions, which, were too wild to come even close to where Vince was. He directed two more rounds to the window in order to break the glass. Taking a run, putting his elbows first, he jumped though the broken window, got up and ran through the back neighbor's yards, till he reached the back street and his car, driving away with the screech of the tires.

Dr. Thurston was near that window but crouched as the bullets broke the glass of it and Leopold almost fell on top of him.

Before the doctor could react, Leopold had hit him in the face, run through the alley, jumped the fence at the back of the house, and disappeared into the dark.

Vince had opened the front door for Silvia and the Doctor, and they all ran to attend to Laura, who was semiconscious and bleeding profusely from the stab wound.

"She is alive but has been hurt badly. One of you get me some rags, sheets, whatever to put pressure on her wound, and the other call 911," said Dr. Thurston.

"She is trying to say something," said General Silvia Fuentes. Laura was pale as a ghost and obviously bleeding inside but managed to say, "Scarface man, after Kelly." Then she passed out.

"That man was after Kelly Carter, as we suspected. I don't know if this woman knows where she is, but she gave Kelly the senator's number, and it would have been easy for him and whoever sent him to put two and two together. You two better call Jason to warn him and get there fast. I'll stay with this poor woman and meet you at the Senator's later. Oh, and neither one of you was ever here tonight. I am a friend of the family who came to visit and was fortunate enough to stop the crime. Go now."

The Police and ambulance sirens could be heard when Vince and Silvia drove away.

Chapter 14
THE PLAN

After making the call, Vince gave Silvia directions to the Senator's home. They arrived in less than fifteen minutes. The senator was not home yet, but Jason told them that he had been informed of the attack on Laura Mason and the fact that Doctor Thurston stayed with her and was riding in the ambulance to the nearest hospital. The doctor had said that her injury looked very serious, and it was possible that she may be dead as they spoke.

The senator told them that he was coming home as soon as possible and to tell Jason to be vigilant—an obvious unnecessary precaution as Jason was already ready, holding a Glock pistol and an AR-15 rifle. General Silvia had a 9mm Beretta, and Vince had earlier been given a Colt 45 pistol. Additionally, Jason had two shotguns on top of the coffee table in the living room.

General Silvia could only smile while saying: "OMG, looks like we are ready for a full-scale war," and asked Vincenso, "What do you think of this, Lieutenant?"

"Well General Graham," he responded, "there have been already three casualties related to this affair so far today, and the night is young. The man, or men, who are doing this are not going to rest until everyone who is aware of the plot is neutralized, especially Mrs. Carter, and she is here, in this house."

"You are absolutely correct, Lieutenant; I know Masters, and he will not go down easily and certainly not without a fight. I am sure the man with the scar that Mrs. Mason mentioned works for him. Most likely, he has others to do his dirty work, not to mention the soldiers under his command who, although not involved in this shit, are supposed to obey his orders without question. Good thing Flynn Masters now has a desk job. But still, he is a general of the US armed forces, and the Chief of Staff. So, let's be prepared for the worst while hoping for the best. Meanwhile, I will call some friends."

The voice on the other end of the phone sounded sleepy when she answered the phone.

"Hello Karla, you sound sleepy. Hope I did not get you out of bed."

"Who the hell is this? It is almost eleven p.m., and no, I was not in bed, just watching the news and getting ready to call the day."

"I'm sorry, Lioness, this is Tigress, I know that you are retired, married, a mommy, and owner of both a preschool and a martial arts school for kids, but we really need you to help us."

"Shit, Silvia, I am retired and a mother of two kids, and who is this 'us' that you need me to help?"

"It is 'U-S,' Karla. Yes, as in the United States, and it concerns a matter of national security, A very serious matter of National Security. Besides, all we need you for is to babysit someone important and to bail someone you know out of jail."

"Who and who, Silvia?"

"Sorry Karla, I cannot give you the first who, but the second who is our old friend Badger."

"Richard Boone? I thought he was dead."

"No names, please. Yes Badger almost drank himself to death several times. But this time he is in jail here in DC, apparently for something related to a bar brawl in which a cop ended up with a broken something. You may need to post bail and-or use your charm to get him out. We will pay you back as soon as possible and add a bonus for your inconvenience."

"I think I will use my charm. It will be cheaper. But I will take the bonus as long as it does not come out of your pocket."

"Most likely won't come out of my pocket. I'm working with very rich people here. One more thing, dear, as soon as you get him bring him to my apartment and wait for me there."

Thereafter General Graham dialed another number, this

time the one of the stockade at the nearby military base. She requested to speak with the officer in charge. Once she was connected, she identified herself and gave some orders to the officer on duty. Then she said to Vince, "Lieutenant, I am afraid that you have to wear your uniform, at least for tonight. We will need to pick someone at the base and you will have to be his guardian angel."

"I am afraid that I do not have my uniform nearby, General, the closest I have to a uniform are my fatigues."

"Those will do. And also, we need to move Mrs. Carter out of here. Even if the Mason woman did not reveal to her attacker the name of the person whose phone number she wanted, whoever he was took Mrs. Mason's phone and it would not take much to locate this house."

"Do you seriously think they would dare to attack the home of a US senator, especially someone as prominent and popular as Senator McClain?"

"I think they would not need to use force. That would be stupid. Especially since they can do it legally, sending the FBI or even the local police looking for Mrs. Carter. Remember that they have publicly labeled her as a deranged, disturbed, and delusional person? They may even assert that she is a danger to herself and-or others. Any judge would sign a search warrant under those premises."

At that very moment, the senator walked through the door and said: "I heard what the general said, and I agreed two hundred percent with her. Mrs. Carter needs to move out of this house as soon as possible, but we also need to plan what to do thereafter." He continued, "First of all, I think everyone will be safer as more people are aware of the situation, and I am not only talking about us present here but the American and the Chinese people as well.

"I have informed several senators and congresspersons of The problem—and I am happy to say—that most apparently believed that the danger was real and that Kelly Carter was telling the truth. However, I regret that most of those were not members of my own party and therefore, at least in part, politically motivated.

"They will launch an investigation and probably start impeachment procedures. However, we will need witnesses, and the best will be the woman and the Chinese scientists.

"So first of all, right now, I am going to call some members of the press who I am friendly with and arrange for a press conference first thing in the morning here at my house. Meanwhile, the rest of you should try to secure Dr. DelToro and Dr. Chin Ghan Do.

"I will stay here with my wife and Jason to greet the search party that POTUS and his generals may be assembling now. Also, I prefer not to know where you are taking, Mrs. Carter."

Talking to his wife, the senator added, "Dear, would you be so kind as to wake our guest up and get her ready for a short ride inside the trunk of the general's car?" Then, returning to address the rest of them, the senator said, "The woman doctor is known to work best at night and with very few assistants. Therefore, chances are she will be at her lab. Dr. Joe Thurston would have free access to the hospital and the labs…Where is he at this moment?"

"He stayed with Mrs. Mason and said he was going to ride in the ambulance with her to the hospital.…We do not know which hospital, but I have his cell number. I can call him," said General Fuentes.

"With some luck, they took her to the same hospital where the virus is, and we can meet him there and go for the woman and the virus," said Vince.

"That would certainly be lucky, but the labs are at Walter Reed and most civilians are not taken there…. Yet, you never know with Joe. If he was able to make super soldiers out of common grunts, he can do anything. No offense intended, Lieutenant," said the Senator

"None taken, Senator. Speaking of which, aren't those the pictures of the grunts turned super soldiers that Dr. Thurston brought here earlier? Can I look at them. Maybe the guy who attacked Mrs. Mason is one of them? I'll do it while Mrs. Carter gets ready to go," Vince said, pointing to the boxes with files on the dining room table.

He barely had glanced at a couple of the pictures, discarding the ones that had crosses on top, indicating that they were in a better world before he said, "I've seen this guy. He lives in the tents. He's high on dope or booze most of the time. I never guessed he has the same curse that I have"

General Fuentes said, "It is a curse only if you are not able to control it. So far it seems that you are doing okay. Let me see that picture for a moment, please."

She glanced at the picture and said: "OMG, that is Rabbit. Thurston said he was living with the homeless, but he thought he was in Florida. When did you see him last, Vince?"

It was the first time since they met that she called him by his name, and he definitely liked it.

"I can't be sure, but may be less than a week ago."

"Great, maybe we can track him down and make him part of the team."

At this point, a still sleepy Kelly Carter came down the stairway.

"Guess you are ready to go, good luck and good hunting. Oh, almost forgot, here is the address of the Chinese doctor. He lives in an apartment with his wife and a daughter." The senator said this while handling a piece of paper to the general.

And then all left the senator's home.

Chapter 15
MASTER'S MASTER PLAN

"So, the little rat may have found shelter at the home of Senator James McClain? It makes sense. He is another rat, unfortunately, a much more powerful one," said General Masters to Leopold.

And then he added, "That woman, Laura, won't be able to recognize you, right? Are you sure you killed her, Leopold?"

"As sure as I am talking to you now, General. I put this knife right into her chest". Leopold shows the General his weapon.

They were meeting at a semi-abandoned warehouse, which supposedly harbored an automobile repair shop, but mostly was used by Leopold as his operation center. Most of the automobiles there were useless and rusty. Although, more often than not, friends of Leopold brought in stolen vehicles to be cut and sold for parts to be shipped overseas. Drugs coming from Mexico and South America were also received to be re-shipped and distributed. Leopold was smart enough not to take direct part in most of those dealings and made his profit by renting the warehouse temporarily and for very high fees to the people involved in the trade.

This was General Masters' first time at "the shop," and he was not very comfortable with it. Yet the place was much less conspicuous than meeting with Leopold at either one of their homes or at the general's office.

"I can get in that senator's home easy and extract her or kill her," said Leopold.

"Are you stupid or what? You are talking about doing a home invasion at the house of a prominent US senator. If the woman is there, she has told him everything she knows, and who knows how many more people are now aware of the situation."

He did not mention to Leopold what the "situation" really

was because he did not know how the Russian would react. Besides, it was top secret, and the President had put the whole operation on halt.

Masters did not tell Leopold that the President was involved and that he was being paid with taxpayers' money. All he said was repeating what had been in the news: that the woman had gone to bunkers, had become a turncoat, and possessed information vital to National Security.

"We have the homes of all the politicians opposed to the President under surveillance, and they are supposed to report if our lady shows at the door of any of them. So far, nothing. But let me try to get in contact with the team watching the home of this particular senator. We can do this legally if we have enough evidence to show that she is there. We'll get an order from a judge and send the local police to search the house."

It took General Flynn Masters a few minutes to get in contact with the agents watching the home of Senator McClain, and after he got a report from them, he just said, "Shit."

"What is it, General?" inquired Leopold.

"They report not having seen the lady in question but that there has been a lot of activity in the place. Several vehicles have been coming in and out of the house and they've seen at least one woman getting into the compound. This is the picture they took and are running through the scanners at headquarters now."

Masters stopped as his cell phone rang. "Give me a second. I have to take this most important call now."

It was the President asking for a report, and after listening for a few seconds, followed by another few seconds of silence, the President said, "She is there all right. It may be too late, but I am calling a judge friend of mine to get a search warrant. Meanwhile, make sure you secure the doctors."

After saying, "Yes, Sir," Flynn went back to Leopold. "My boss will take care of the search of the senator's home. Meanwhile, I want you to go fetch the other two people and take them to a safe, secure location. You will not use force unless strictly necessary. But, if you meet outside interference, you are authorized to neutralize the targets whoever they are. Take as many men as you need. I am putting the pictures of the subjects and likely locations on this nontraceable cell phone."

Leopold looked at the pictures "To get a Chinaman and an old lady, I don't think I need much help, General."

"Never underestimate the situations. Didn't they teach you that in the Russian Military intelligence, my dear Leopold? I guess you never were good at that business, were you?"

The general loved to put people down, especially people beneath him whom he could control, and he thought that Leopold was one of those. He did not know that Leopold had had " the enhancing serum," and while he had only one dose out of three usually required, he was no longer the man he brought from Afghanistan. Leopold did not appreciate the general's remarks but swallowed his pride and said nothing.

"Oh, one more thing, Leo. If you do not find the lady doctor at her home, go to the virology lab at Walter Reed. She may be there. I have doubled the guard at that lab right now. However, if you call me before going there, I can call my guys off so you can get in without any problem. And here, Leo, use this key as an ID and to open as many doors as you find closed before reaching the laboratory." He gave Leopold an ID electronic card. "This will open all the doors at the hospital. Please try your best not to be messy."

Leopold Mishanivich hated to be called Leo. He knew the general was aware of that dislike. His distrust of him grew larger as he thought: if they only need that Lady because she has become a traitor and a threat to National Security, why they need to use me, instead of the FBI or the CIA?. There is something more obscure and stinky in this whole thing, perhaps I should get that lady myself and get some answers. But then he looked at Flynn Masters and decided it was safer to play his game….at least for the time being.

With this, they both left the place and went in different directions.

Leopold collected two men in whom he had confidence, and, in a stolen commercial van, they departed to fulfill the orders from General Flynn Masters, who, once in his car, called the President again.

"My men are on their way to fetch the targets sir. Do you have any new orders?"

"Yes, General, I do. When your men find the subjects, tell them to make sure that they ask them to get the virus and destroy any evidence of it. If they can transfer the virus to a secure and safe location, tell them it is okay to preserve it; if not, they should also destroy the virus."

"Do you want us to eliminate the subjects, sir?"

"Not yet; they are more useful alive and denying everything than dead and raising suspicions. But eventually, and unfortunately, it may come to that."

"Very well, sir. Good night."

"It is not going to be a good night, Masters. I probably won't be able to take a wink unless we find the Carter woman and silence her."

"Has the judge signed the search warrant yet, sir?"

"The son of a bitch was already in bed, but he got up and is on his way to issue the warrant. The senator's home will be searched within the hour. I want you to come to the White House to plan our next move and work on damage control in case this unfortunate incident is made public."

"I am on my way."

Chapter 16
THE WOMEN AT WORK

General Silvia Graham-Fuentes entered her apartment accompanied by Vince and Kelly Carter. Nobody else had arrived there so far, so Silvia called her friend Karla Messer, aka Lioness, to inquire about her progress in bailing out Richard "the Badger" Bone.

Karla reported that, unfortunately, that very same morning, the Badger had been sentenced to six months in federal prison. He was due to be transferred out of the County Jail the following morning. She said that she would have to use both her charm and money to get him out.

Silvia said that money was not a problem, but she needed him tonight before he was sent away.

"I see what I can do. If I am not there within the hour, neither charm nor money have worked." Karla hung up.

Thereafter, Silvia called Dr. Thurston, who gave her the news that Laura Mason was still in surgery, but the surgeons had told him that her wounds were not life-threatening and that she would survive.

Her husband and children had been informed, and they had arrived at the hospital. He would leave the hospital soon and join them at Silvia's apartment.

Silvia explained to the doctor that she could not leave Kelly alone. She was going to call a couple of soldiers under her command to guard her. She hated to do that, but it would be for a short time, only until he or her friend Karla arrived. Meanwhile, she will go with Vincenso to try to extract James Timberlake, aka "Moose," from the stockade.

Dr. Thurston gave General Fuentes the good news that Kirk White, aka "Wolf," another one of the subjects who had received the full three doses of the enhancing serum several years before, had also been located.

Thurston had made some calls while waiting at the

hospital and had learned that "Wolf" had been arrested late the night before for crashing a military jeep against the entrance of a military base while stone drunk. He was likely in the same location as "The Moose."

"That is good news, Doctor. We will try to get both of them at the same time. I was going to give Karla one hour to get here before calling the base to send me the soldiers, this is an unofficial business and I hate to implicate the men under my command in it, but if you can get here sooner, you can stay with the Carter woman, and give Karla all the time she needs"

"I will be there in less than half an hour. Traffic is light tonight in DC."

Karla Messer was a beautiful woman, five foot seven inches of pure muscle distributed artistically in the proper places in her body, a body that made men turn their heads when she passed by—and women hated her for that. She had feline, charming, dark green eyes and raven black hair that she let grow below her shoulders and usually kept in a ponytail, except in cases when she wanted to charm men to get what she wanted of them.

In addition, she had the attributes of being clever, brilliant, and very resourceful. She was capable of negotiating under the most dire, difficult situations, and was fluent in at least four languages. Thus, the mission she had been assigned that night seemed like a piece of cake, up until she learned that nobody had paid the bail for the Badger and he had been sitting in the county jail for almost a month, until that very same morning when the Judge gave him a six months sentence to be served in a federal prison…, So, it was too late to get him out on bail, so, she decided to use her charm and her money.

She became tearful in front of the only three officers that were on duty at the small County jail, telling them that Badger was her fiancée, that he had disappeared on the very day they were going to get married, that she only had very recently learned the reason he abandoned her at the altar was because he was in arrested and put in jail. Most likely, he had a bachelor's party and got drunk. The poor guy was not a habitual drinker and had difficulty holding his alcohol when he drank too much.

At this point, she had the officers on the verge of tears, but they still wouldn't release the prisoner. He was officially a federal prisoner now, and there was nothing they could do.

Then came the offer: $5000 apiece if they let her brothers bust him out of jail. Nobody would know anything. They could erase the part of the tape showing her ever having been at the police station.

"That is, of course, if you have a camera here, like they show in the movies. Then two of my brothers can come with guns- of course unloaded- and you let them handcuff you and rescue my little Ricky. What do you say, fifteen thousand dollars in one night, five thousand a piece. Is not that about what you make in a month"?

The three guys did not hesitate to accept her offer.

Of course, she did not have that much money on her, but after going to the nearest ATM, she came back and gave them one thousand dollars each.

"My brothers will give you the rest when they get here…less than an hour, I promised; thank you guys, you are the greatest," and she left after giving each of the officers a kiss on the cheek.

Then she called her husband on her cell and explained the situation. "Leave the kids with the neighbor. I need you and your brother, a stolen car, and thirteen thousand dollars."

After listening to some curse words over the phone, the husband agreed.

After all, he was also an ex-Marine and an extreme games practitioner in addition to teaching at the karate school they owned.

After less than half-hour they showed up at the corner driving a beat-up Toyota, extended cabin truck.

She took the driver's seat, put the money in three different envelopes, and told them to put on ski masks and gloves and make sure that their guns were unloaded. She did not want any unforeseen accidents and certainly no victims.

Everything went according to plan. The guys walked in, pointed their guns at the officers, handcuffed them to chairs and took the keys to the cells. They asked the prisoners which of them was Richard Boone, aka the Badger. Although he was somewhat scared at first, the prospect of getting out of there instead of going to prison was almost too good to believe.

They got away with the prisoner and, as they boarded the Toyota with their guns still in the back of the Badger, she poked her head out of the car and said, "Remember me, Badger? Don't be afraid we are friends. Drive us to my car. It's around the corner. Drop this piece of junk and go back to the house. You guys did a great job."

"Fuck, it was too easy, and it was a lot of fun," said one of the guys without removing the ski mask.

"Yes, a very expensive kind of fun," said her husband. "Where are you going now?"

"Badger and I are going to see the Tigress. I may be late tonight, or early tomorrow. It all depends on whatever she has in mind"

Her husband just grunted another "fuck" under the mask and drove away saying, "I love you, but I want my money back."

When they arrived at the Tigress apartment, Dr. Thurston was already there, and after hugging each other and the Badger, Silvia made a brief introduction, with special emphasis on Kelly Carter:

"I imagine, if you watch the news, you know who this lady is. And, after hearing her story, you'll see why it is so important to keep her safe and in one piece. I would love to do it myself because she can be charming, but we have to go spring two other friends from the stockade and to fetch two others folks that are not expected to be so friendly."

After Karla told them the story of the extraction of the Badger, it drew laughs from those presents. Silvia said to all: "I owe you big time, friend, and your money shall be returned with a bonus added. However, after you learn the story from Mrs. Carter, you will see how serious shit this is and why we need assets we can trust, and assets who we know can kick ass better than most."

And after a brief pause, she added, "Even if we are a little older and rustier than in the good old times".

"First item of the night will be to spring the Moose and the Wolf from the stockade at the base. Badger and I should be able to do that without much trouble. First, though, we need to fit him with military fatigues...I think I can help with that. A friend of mine changes clothes here from time to time." She went into her bedroom to look in her closet.

Karla and Doctor Thurston smiled at hearing that. The others did not get it.

After a few minutes, Silvia returned with some military fatigues and said, "It may be a bit big for you, Badger, but those will have to do. Karla, you stay here with Mrs. Carter and guard her with your life. Here is a weapon in case you do not have one." She handed her a 9mm Beretta.

"Thank you, Silvia. I prefer to carry my own," Karla said, as she pulled a 9mm Sig-Sauer from her belt.

"Very well then. I suggest that the doctor and the lieutenant go fetch the lady doctor, we will go get the Chinese man after we get Wolf and Moose. I do not trust those Chinese. They all seem to know karate and are very good fighters. Hopefully we would not need to use force...but you never know."

"Whether the lady doctor is at her apartment or at the hospital lab, she may be well guarded, and so will be the Chinese doctor. I am going to stop at the hospital lab where they experiment with animals and get a couple of the sedating darts guns they use to control the chimps. Perhaps I should see if they have more than one. You could use that with the Chinaman," said Doctor Thurston.

"That is a great idea, but I am afraid there is not enough time. We have to do this tonight before the President and General Masters extract or kill those two targets," responded Silvia.

"Did you say the President and General Masters, General Silvia...what do they have to do with this?" Those were questions asked almost simultaneously by Karla and the Badger

Percy D. Kepfer

"Karla, you will understand after Mrs. Carter here tells her story to Badger and you. I will brief you in the way over to the base. Right now I am going to step into my office to write the release order for Timberland and White."

Chapter 17
THE CHINESE SCIENTIST

The release of Moose and Wolf went rather smoothly, as the MPs at the stockade seemed to be glad to get rid of the men. They said to Badger:

"We hope the General knows what she is getting into. Those two are trouble. We hope she sends them someplace far away from here."

To which Badger, who was a guy of few words, just responded, "I'm guessing she knows." He signaled to the two prisoners not to acknowledge that they knew him while still in the building where the guards could hear them. He just pushed the two men ahead of him and walked to the car parked several meters from the gate.

Once outside, of course, they had all kinds of questions for him, especially why and for what the general needed them.

Answer: "The general will tell you shortly"

"The general, what general, is he here?'" both said

Answer "Is not a he. The general is a she."

The car was Karla's and the inside lights did not turn on when they opened the doors. Nevertheless, they both immediately recognized General Silvia Fuentes-Graham, their ex-commander.

"Hello boys, we have some work to do, and you better do it right and willingly and may earn a reward, or I will bring your sore asses back to the stockade, or worse yet, I may put a bullet in your heads. And speaking of heads, for guys who are supposed to be smarter and better than the average GI, you have fucked up your lives pretty badly. How many promotions and demotions have you had...eight or ten? It's got to be a record."

"It is not our fault, General Fuentes. It's due to that damn serum they injected us with," Wolf said.

"Bullshit, you both, I have the same serum, and I have done better than most men in the ranks," said Fuentes.

"With all due respect to the general that may be because you are a woman, and the women tolerated that shit better," said the Moose.

"Bullshit again, Moose, several of the women who got the serum died. That's why the government stopped giving it. At least I hope they did stop."

"Sorry, boss. We did not know that."

"Well, now you know and, if all goes well you may be able to ask more questions and get more answers from a person who is the real expert on what's in that medication.

"Now we have to focus. We are going across the river to the home of a Chinese man to extract him and bring him to a secure location. I warn you: there may be guards and some other bad people interested in the same person.

You should keep absolute secrecy. This is a matter of serious National Security. People at the highest level of government are involved.... So what we are about to do may not be totally legal. Are you with us, or would you prefer to return to the stockade?"

The two men just looked at Badger for some kind of guide or response, but he just shrugged his shoulders, played with the 9mm pistol in his hand, and said, "She knows what she is doing. Karla is also in".

Silvia briefed the men of the situation as they drove out of Andrews Air Force base and exited into 95/495, heading across the river to Alexandria, the area where the residence of Doctor Chin-Ghan-Do was supposed to be located, somewhere near the Landmark Mall.

Traffic was light at that hour, and most businesses and restaurants were closed or closing. Using the car GPS, it took a relatively short time to get to the area.

Not soon after arriving, their collective instincts told them that something was wrong. They spotted two black SUVs, with their tires screeching, pulling away from the front of one house, which had the front door wide open.

Silvia hesitated between following the cars or going into

the house and then decided for the latter and pulled over at the site where the SUVs had been parked.

"Badger, give Moose and Wolf a weapon," she ordered, and then said, "We are going in. Moose and Wolf, take the back. Badger and I are going through the front door."

They went in, and as soon as Silvia looked inside the house, she saw all in disarray: broken lamps and ornaments, overturned chairs, and a man lying on the floor with blood pouring out of several wounds on his chest and abdomen. She had seen enough dead people to know the man was a corpse.

Telling Badger not to touch anything, she walked further into the house and found another dead person. This one was a young woman, shot in the center of the forehead.

"We were too late," she lamented and was ready to get out when she heard quiet sobs coming from the top of a stairwell; she went up, and there was a six or seven-year-old Asian-looking girl, who appeared to be very, very scared.

Silvia put her gun out of sight and, with soothing words, climbed the stairs. She was instantly confronted by the girl, now yielding a baseball bat and trying to swing at her.

Silvia took the bat easily from her and held her in her arms while speaking softly: "I am not going to hurt you, little one. Do not be afraid."

The girl let Silvia hold her as she cried inconsolable on her shoulders.

"Do you speak English, little girl? Do you understand me? What is your name?"

Between sobs, the girl answered as they came down the stairs. Silvia did her best to cover the girl's eyes, so she would not see the bodies of her parents.

"My name is Lianhua, which means Lotus Flower in Chinese. The bad guys hurt my dad and my mummy…. I am scared."

"Yes, sweetheart, I am afraid they did hurt your parents. But you'll be okay now, I will take care of you and keep the bad guys away," Silvia said, holding the little girl, kissing her forehead, and walking with her out of the house.

"You speak very good English for a little girl. You must

be very smart," said Silvia.

"I am American. I was born right here, but I do speak Chinese too," the girl said, proudly still between sobs.

"See, I knew you were a smart girl, and I am not as clever as you are," said Silvia

By then, Richard Boone, the Badger, had finished searching around the house and was joined by Kirk White, the Wolf, and James Timberlake, the Moose. They all had the same comment and the same question: "The Place is a mess; we got to get out of here before the cops come, and what about the girl? What are we going to do with her?"

"The girl stays with me…with us, and that is an order," said Silvia with a broken voice

"What is wrong with the general?" Moose asked. "I never saw her like that."

"She is a woman. Underneath all that toughness and bravado, she is still a woman, and women have maternal instincts and sensitivity," Badger responded.

"I guess that makes her human. Funny, I never thought of her like that."

That moment granted General Silvia Fuentes-Graham, a multi-decorated US Army legend, further respect and admiration from guys who already had a great deal of respect and admiration for their commander.

"Okay, fellows, let's get out of here, and do not forget that we still have work to do. We're going back to my apartment. I have to put this princess to bed. I am sure it is past her bedtime. Are you hungry, Lianhua?"

"No, I just want my mummy and daddy." She began to cry again.

They got in the car. This time she let Badger drive. Timberlake rode shotgun and Silvia, holding the girl, sat in the back with Wolf.

"You know, Lianhua, that I am not as smart as you are, so I have a little trouble saying your name. Would it be okay if I called you Lia from now on?"

The girl just nodded a yes while they drove on, both girls with tears in their eyes.

Nevertheless, while holding the girl—who was beginning to nod to sleep—Silvia dialed 911 using a burner phone and disguising her voice. Asking for the police, she explained that she was walking her dog when she saw a couple of cars speeding away and leaving the door of the home open.

She told the 911 operator that she had peeked through the door and seen two people lying on the floor with lots of blood around them.

Then she dialed Dr. Thurston and reported what happened.

The doctor gave her better news: The Patels had been able to locate Dr. Del Toro's phone number and found out that she was not in her apartment but at the laboratory at Walter Reed. He, Vincent, and Rabbit—yes Rabbit—who the Patels had also been able to locate Leroy Smith, who was no longer homeless. He was working at a computer store. Computers, electronics, and explosives were his thing. He was long term customer of Patel's internet bar and, in fact, they were instrumental in getting him a job. He said he was willing to come on board.

Dr. Thurston and the team were currently en route to the hospital, having taken the proactive step of securing an ambulance for the urgent situation.

"By the way, I have some good news. Laura Mason had had surgery, and the surgeons said that she would be okay."

They hoped there would be no significant problems in extracting the scientist and that she would still be a member of the world by the time they arrived.

Chapter 18
BAD NEWS REPORTS

General Charles Flynn Masters went from pale to livid, sweaty to cold, scratching and at times pulling at his scanty, almost white hair. He also paced the floor and kicked chairs and furniture. A few times, he almost dropped or threw the cell phone he was using.

He was a tall man at 6 feet, 1 inch. In spite of his age—almost 65—he was straight as a rod and walked with a wide strut, so military that anyone could quickly tell his profession just by watching him walk. He was an imposing man with a face that seemed chiseled in granite and expressionless eyes, that, if anything, suggested a cruel soul, or a total lack of one.

Indeed, he had a reputation for his cruelty, having shown plenty of that during his tours in Afghanistan and Iraq, where he showed pleasure in torturing prisoners and suspected enemy combatants. He was certainly not loved by the men under his command, and the only reason nobody had shot him in the back was that he was smart enough to surround himself with a handful of men whom he allowed to pillage, rob and rape—and be rewarded for doing it. He called them "his loyal dogs." Leopold had become one of them, for some time at least, after he saved him from being shot by his Soviet comrades.

Though General Charles Flynn Masters was a West Point man who had seen action in the Middle East, he was never distinguished for doing anything special nor for any act of valor. His ascension through the ranks was obtained mainly by deception, by kissing a lot of asses, and by the influence of his uncle, a now-deceased US senator, along with the money of his wealthy father, who had sent him to boarding school in Westchester, New York, were he met the man who was now the President of the United States of America.

Masters was a couple of years younger than POTUS, but

because both came from the same area of New York City. They were roommates and were very similar in character—with the exception that Masters was not a coward and POTUS was. Thus, they connected from day one.

POTUS, at the time, was a student and fellow who was bullied by most of the students. He survived only thanks to the generous allowance he got from his father, which allowed him to pay his tormentors in exchange for leaving him alone.

That changed when Masters arrived at the school; He offered protection in exchange for the money he was paying to other students. Of course, he had to break some noses, produce many black eyes and kick some butts in order to assure the physical well-being of his friend.

Flynn did not need the friend's money. He came from a wealthy family. His grandfather had made tons of money selling arms and goods to countries at war—at very inflated prices. Masters was the only son, so he expected to be the substantial heir to the family fortune.

Unfortunately for young Charles F. Masters, his father, unlike his grandfather, was an honorable man. He did not continue his father's business and instead invested in the stock market, making lots of money and then losing it all during the stock market collapse. His father died of a stroke, in no small part due to the loss of his fortune, though his son's carefree behavior may have been contributory.

After his father died, whatever was left of the family fortune was given to a sister younger than him, who was a war widow. Only a paltry amount of the family fortune, plus a hefty amount from his father's life insurance, went to Charles. Nevertheless, most of the money was rapidly squandered by the young Charles, mostly through gambling but also splurged on women and expensive cars.

General Charles Masters' uncle, a brother of his father, was a young US senator who was rapidly becoming a star in the ranks of his party in Washington. He was left with the responsibility of taking care of Charles and his sister, a task that, in addition to his political career and family life, was indeed a very heavy burden. Therefore, he used his influence and got Charles Flynn Masters admitted to West Point.

After graduation, he remained in contact with his roommate, and when he later became President, he chose Masters to be his Chief of Staff. POTUS, by then, had also lost most of his fortune, in crazy inversions that led to several bankruptcies.

So both POTUS and Masters needed money. They needed it badly. POTUS knew he had no chance of being re-elected and had several multimillion lawsuits pending against him, plus three ex-wives to support. Masters had mounting gambling debts and two ex-wives to support. So, when they were briefed about the virus and the vaccine, they immediately saw the potential for making billions of dollars.

General Charles F. Masters was ruthless, cruel, ambitious, and above all totally without scruples, the kind of man that would not blink an eye to commit genocide, or in this case, xenocide. He was the perfect partner for the President's plan with the deadly virus.

That night, General Masters, wearing a civilian raincoat over old military fatigues, was very, very upset. He talked on his cell phone and kept kicking things until he hurt his right foot and screamed.

"What do you mean that the Chinese doctor is dead? How? Why? All you were asked to do was to get him and bring him here, without harm, without violence. What the hell happened?"

"…Oh, I see, he became aggressive. He knew karate. I am assuming you idiots did not knock gently on his door or rang the bell and ask politely to come with you, did you.? Or you broke his door and came inside his home, guns blaring and shouting obscenities?"

There was no response from the other side of the phone and Masters understood that the later scenario was the one had taken place.

"What, his wife took part in the fray, and you shot her? OMG! She knew karate as well? And after you killed the husband, you had to kill her anyway so she wouldn't identify you by your fucken scars."

"Now do tell me that you have the woman doctor and are bringing her here."

Silence on the other side of the phone

"Oh, she was not there. Do you mean in her apartment? Did you check the lab at the hospital?"

Leopold replied from the other end of the phone: "Yes, she was there but had some seizure and was rushed to the emergency room, and from there, she disappeared. Apparently, she was taken home by ambulance, but we went back there, and she is not near it."

"Shit, shit, shit.... You fucked up this time, Leo. You do not even have an idea of how bad you fucked up this time; this is bad, bad, super bad. Stay wherever you are and try not to leave a body trail behind you. I am sending a cleanup crew to the home of the Chinese. I hope the cops have not been called yet. Otherwise, you and I will be in seriously deep shit."

Masters, of course, never thought of blaming himself for not telling Leopold that the person who needed to talk to the Chinese doctor was nobody else but the president of the United States of America. Had he known that he would have come willfully and peacefully with Leo.

But the General was not the kind of person who felt guilt, remorse, or offered an admission of error.

Chapter 19
THE DOCTOR GETS THE DOCTOR

Doctor Joe Thurston, Vincenso Batagliari, and the newest recruited member of the team, Leroy Smith, code name "Rabbit," were raiding an ambulance. Rabbit was at the wheel.

Rabbit was a small-framed guy, perhaps 5 foot 5, with a weight of no more than 135 pounds on his best days. He wore thick glasses and, although he was dark-skinned, he was not black. Rabbit regarded himself as a "Pacific Islander." He wore an Afro-curly black haircut, somewhat short so as not to appear that he had come to the 21 Century straight from the 1960s. He was shy and friendly, smiled frequently and laughed like a teenager. However, his looks were deceiving, as he was extremely smart. His IQ, having been tested upon enrollment in the army, scored over 180. Leroy's specialty was electronics, mechanics, and anything related to machines, cars, airplanes, helicopters, and explosives.

Leroy had had no behavior problems. However, he had been dishonorably discharged from the Army and almost court marshalled because he had the habit of hacking into the computer systems of the Pentagon, the FBI, the CIA and Homeland Security, among other places, and selling information to whomever was interested in buying it.

Rabbit was not a traitor, he loved his country and had fought for it, being smart enough to sell only information that he considered benign and unimportant. He had the ability to make it look top secret and often actually sold false information.

That lasted until he was caught and served three of five years in federal prison. Upon his release his family did not want to see him and it was very difficult for him to find employment until he met the Patels at their internet café. They got him a job at an electronics store belonging to a friend of theirs. Rabbit did smoke weed and had a line of cocaine once in a while, but he was not an addict. Heck nobody is perfect!

Dr Thurston knew the whole pack and their stories because he had been, along with his colleagues Neil Pratt and Bruce Colton, the developers and administrators of the "Enhancement Serum" and had been following her progress and problems for several years

They were now driving through Bethesda, Maryland, and approaching the Tri-service Walter Reed National Military Medical Center at 8901 Rockville Pike, Drive. Thurston instructed his companions to leave him in the back of the hospital, park the ambulance in front of the ER, and wait for him.

Before leaving the ambulance, he carefully checked the pistol that fired the sedating darts and made sure that he had at least three usable darts. It turned out he had five, so he put them in the small case and slipped them into his pocket. He also made sure that the mini-tape recorder and his cell phone were working properly.

Thurston was a member of the hospital's medical staff, although he rarely practiced medicine and had no direct contact with patients anymore. For the last several years, he has dedicated himself to research and investigation. As such, he had a laboratory in the basement, which was the site of most research laboratories, including Dr. DelToro's.

He used his ID card to open the door and walked a long corridor. He took a stairwell to the basement. Sure enough, there was light at DelToro's lab. So, pretending to open his office, he timed the rotation of the few security cameras and walked over to her office with his back to the cameras.

Thurston was somewhat surprised to see that there were only two soldiers on guard, one on each side of the door of Lidia DelToro Lab. They both had batons, though only one had a side arm. Thurston assumed they were MPs. The soldiers had been given chairs to sit in, and both looked very sleepy and bored. No surprise there, as it was almost midnight.

Dr. Thurston decided to forget about secrecy and instead take a casual approach. Therefore, he walked straight to the guards, showed them his credentials, and easily entered Lidia's lab.

She was alone, and there were no guards inside.

Lidia DelToro was a petite woman of Spanish descent, now in her late forties, who had elevated herself from the hoods of Hialeah in Miami to attend Harvard Medical School, where she graduated *summa cum laude* before becoming a Rhodes Scholar and being considered for a Nobel Prize for her work on virology. The price Lidia paid for that success was loneliness, bitterness, and the absence of love in her life.

Lidia DelToro was perhaps 5 foot-5 inches tall, wore thick spectacles and had black, curly hair that always appeared to be in need of a comb. To top that, she had suffered from severe acne during her adolescence and her face still had some of the scars from it. However, her features were fine. Behind those spectacles she had a pair of dark big eyes and under the long skirts or pants that she usually wore there was a nicely shaped body, which—it seemed—nobody in Washington had ever seen. Lidia did not smile often, but when she did, she revealed a pretty pair of lips and a perfect set of white teeth.

Thurston started the conversation: "Hello, Dr. DelToro. I am surprised to see you working this late. I came to get some papers from my office, but when I saw the light here, I thought that perhaps this was a good time to ask you for your advice".

"Oh, hello, Dr. Thurston! Yes, I do work late at night often. It is so quiet, and I can get so much more done when there is nobody here.

What kind of advice a reputed fellow like you can possibly obtain from a girl like me?" She said that with a smile, but also with a certain degree of sarcasm and annoyance, which Thurston decided best to ignore.

"Well, I am not sure how to tell you this, because it is supposed to be top secret, but, since I know you are involved in it, here it goes."

Thurston saw Lidia stiffen and started paying much closer attention to the words coming from his mouth.

She said, "Go on."

"As it happened, Dr. DelToro, I was summoned to the White House this afternoon, by none less than the President and apparently General Masters, because he was there as well. They told me about this virus and this vaccine that you and Doctor Chin-Ghan are working on and asked if I would participate in the project. I requested them to allow me to consult my pillow about the matter. They expect an answer from me in the morning. I have to confess that I am intrigued and the reward may be handsome, but I am not sure if I am fitted to do it."

Thurston took the risk of mentioning that he had been allowed to refuse, not knowing if DelToro knew what happened to the two who declined the offer earlier that day.

However, suddenly appearing relaxed, Dr. DelToro said, "You mean you have scruples or perhaps guilt, Dr. Thurston, don't you? You can say no, they will understand. Some of the people who were there this morning declined. However, you will be missing a lifetime opportunity to help humanity, Doctor."

Evidently, Lidia DelToro was not aware of the "tragic accidental demise" of those who declined to participate in the project.

"I am not sure how infecting millions of people with a deathly virus would help humanity, so, please Dr. DelToro, enlighten me and give your advice."

"Dr. Thurston, I know that you do not know much about me, other than perhaps reading my articles and reading about my work with viruses. I was born in a place called Hialeah, which is a poor part of Miami, mostly Cuban at that time. My father was a Cuban immigrant, a disabled veteran from the Angola war. And my mother was an illegal alien from Guatemala. They met in Miami while he was working as a cook and waiter at a Cuban restaurant, and she was the cleaning lady. They fell in love and got married.

"After I was born, an only child, my mother died of

anorexia nervosa, due to postpartum depression when I was only two years old. My dad was devastated but eventually found a woman from Cuba and brought her to live with us. She was not Cinderella's stepmother but neither was she loving and tender towards me and less so, after they had a son, my brother, whom I loved dearly, but one fateful afternoon was struck by a car and died."

"I am sorry to hear that Dr. DelToro. Go on, please," interrupted Thurston.

"Well, even though I was not even present when it happened, it seems this woman, Rita, blamed me and became mean and resentful towards me.

"Although, in honor to the truth, she never got to the point of striking me, there was more verbal abuse. It really hurt because I tried to be the best. I helped around the apartment, learned to cook and made straight As at the school. But it was never good enough.

"Dad was a good man, but he was weak and never had the nerve to stand up for me; I think he suffered from PTSD ever since returning to Cuba from Angola. Also, he was apparently unable to give love to anyone.

"At school, I was really, really good, and I really loved it. I really liked learning, and I never missed a day of school. Of course, I was bullied; not only because I was a straight-A student but also because of my last name—in case you don't know. It means 'Bullfight' in Spanish—and because of my acne and because of my shyness.

"Yet, somehow, I survived. While most kids in my situation got into drugs, alcohol and unlawful things, it was the school that saved me. So I graduated at the top of my class and was the valedictorian year-after-year. Because of my grades and being considered 'a minority,' I was offered all kinds of scholarships to all kinds of schools.

"Of Course, I chose Harvard Medical School, and I graduated from there *summa cum laude*, being then eligible to go to Oxford as a Rhodes Scholar.

"At first, I had plans to return to Hialeah and practice in a poor people's clinic, but then my father died and I had a chance to go with a group of physicians from all over the world to serve in an undeveloped country. I chose Angola.

"I don't know if you have ever been to Africa, Dr. Thurston, but I had never seen so much suffering and so much misery and so much contrast between the rich and the poor as I did see in that country. In my naivety, I thought that those were problems affecting only that country, which, after all, had suffered many years of war. So I visited other countries, I visited India and it was all much of the same: poverty, crime, war, disease, death.

"Still, I thought, 'This is the old continent, and these countries are slowly coming into the 20th Century. This cannot happen in America.'

"So, always traveling on the cheap, and working here and there, for food and shelter mostly, I traveled to Mexico and then South America and, much to my surprise, I found the same thing: sprawling cities; people driving Mercedes along with slums where people starve or kill for food; super elegant shopping malls and boulevards; women dressed with the latest fashions along with people living in huts surviving on corn tortillas—sometimes with rice or beans—and drinking water that, here in the States, you would not use even to wash your butt or bathe your dog.

"There was one thing in common among the poor in all the places I visited: they have children, lots of children. Some tell of having had ten kids and only four or six of them surviving. Those who survive are usually malnourished, sick and infested with worms and other parasites.

"As much as I tried to help and work with several charitable organizations, things were not getting better. It was like a drop in the ocean. Then I realized that, perhaps if these people did not have that many children, fewer women would die in childbirth, leaving behind fewer orphans, and fewer kids would die from infectious diseases.

"Then one day, reading an old magazine, I ran into some population statistics: the world population was—or is—over 8 billion people. That is roughly more than double what it was at the end of the Second World War."

Percy D. Kepfer

"The population of the city capital of Guatemala, where I was at the time, used to be 250,000 in the 60s. It is more than two and a half million now.

"I was aware that I was not discovering anything new. Scientists have been talking about overpopulation for years. Some even call it 'population pollution,' which indeed it is, because the pollution caused by overpopulation is overwhelming and unsustainable.

"I realized, Dr. Thurston, that there are no four horsemen of the Apocalypse. There is only one, and that it is overpopulation by humans who bring about the other four: hunger, war, famine, and death.

"So then I decided to do something about it. I returned to the US and started working to find a way to sterilize as many humans as possible. Obviously, it is impossible to castrate all men or to make all women use contraceptives, especially in the USA. So I started looking for a virus, a virus contagious enough to spread rapidly from person to person and made them sterile.

"At first, I tried with the mumps virus, but not everyone who gets it develops orchitis, and not every orchitis case leads to sterility, so I started to look into other types of Paramyxovirus and other types of viruses until I eventually found something."

Dr. DelToro evidently was passionate about her work, and her story was vivid and most interesting as she came to the point of the deathly virus that Dr. Thurston was concerned about.

"I found this virus, it came from a cave bat and when tried it in rats, it works. It really renders the testicles and the ovaries a hard mass of tissue, totally unable to function normally. Unfortunately, the virus also affects the brain. Therefore, it killed some of the subjects, but not all, not the young and healthy, the ones mostly killed were the old and infirm.

"Yes, I was frustrated, I did not know where to go from there till I read an article from a doctor from China who was working on something similar, so we corresponded. He told

110

me that because the virus was so contagious and lethal, he had developed a vaccine as a precaution in case the virus accidentally spread into the community before we figured a way to control it.

"Unfortunately, I was running out of the grant money that was given to me for the research. So I had to put in a request for additional funds, which of course requires that you give a description of your work in the application. That aroused the interest of the military. The next thing I know is that General Masters comes here. I get the grant, with even more money than I had requested.

"In addition, they flew Doctor Chin-Ghan, the guy I was corresponding with, from China, and settled him here in Washington to work with me with the consent of the Chinese government.

"Obviously, I was delighted. I had plenty of money for my research, and I was going to work with someone I admired and respected and who had similar ideas and interests to mine. However, it never occurred to me to question the motives of the military to support my work.

"It was not until several months later that Masters showed up again and talked about billions of dollars to be made and the good that we would do to the US and the world by 'trimming the herd'—as he put it—after he ran some statistics relating to savings in Medicare, Medicaid, Social Security, and Welfare, to name a few, by eliminating 'in a painless and natural way' the old, the sick, the infirm, the feeble, and sterilizing the rest.

"I have to admit I was horrified and very reluctant to go along with Masters's idea. But after careful thinking, I truly believe that he is right, and it is my patriotic duty to improve this virus and release it to the community. Especially now that I know that the President favors going ahead with it and that we have the vaccine that Dr. Chin developed.

"Seriously, honestly and frankly, I am not interested in all the billions or millions of dollars they expect to make with the vaccine. The virus is right here, in this lab, all twelve vials are in that refrigerator." She pointed to it and walked towards it as she continued talking. "The container will fit in a standard briefcase with some dry ice to keep it cold. And you see those next to it? They are the vials of the vaccine, which all the people involved, including you, Doctor, should get before we release the virus in to the general population.

"The vaccine has been proven to work in humans. The colleagues of Dr. Chin tested it in China, in over 200 people, without any major side effects and resulting in confirmed protection in over 90% of the people."

Thurston asked: "And how was it tested in China, Dr. DelToro"?

She responded, "They gave it to half of the population in two shelters for the elderly—the Chinese equivalent to our nursing homes—one for men and another for women. They made sure that all the nursing, cleaning and management staff were younger than 50 and in good health, then they exposed all to the virus. And, as expected, the younger, unvaccinated people became ill and sterile whereas the vaccinated ones were not affected at all."

"What happened to the elderly and infirm?" asked Thurston.

"I believe most of them died peacefully in their sleep," said Lidia and continued, "So, that is the story in a nutshell, Dr. Thurston. I hope my story helps to convince you to come aboard."

"Your personal story is very interesting and touching, Dr. DelToro. However, the last part and your ideas about using this virus are horrendous. You and your team are trying to play God, or worse, the devil or Hitler. I would not want any part of that horrendous plan, and, in fact, I am going to stop you. I guess you do not know that the two people who refused to take part in this were killed after they left the White House."

"You are lying, Joe Thurston. You are a fool, and you do not realize the good we can do to humanity by eliminating those who are a burden and a drag to civilization and prosperity."

"I think that you are a good person, Doctor Deltoro, but

you also have many misconceptions and have been misled. I do not have the time to convince you to change your mind, therefore you, your virus, and your vaccine are coming with me. Dr. DelToro, I rather you do it voluntarily but I am willing to force you, if necessary," Thurston said while pulling the dart gun from his pocket and pointing it to her.

"What is this? Are you crazy? I'll scream, and the two soldiers guarding the door will arrest you."

"I don't think so, Dr. DelToro. The door is locked and soundproof," said Thurston and he fired a dart directly into her neck.

DelToro whimpered and brought her hand to her neck in a futile effort to remove the dart. Then her legs buckled under her and she began to fall. Thurston anticipated this and caught her in his arms. Then, removing the dart from her neck, he put her gently on top of a desk, fetched the briefcase with the virus and the vaccines, and went out the door to call on the guards.

"Quickly! Come here to help. The Doctor fainted. I know she suffers from seizures and may be having one. Please help me carry her. Bring a stretcher or a wheelchair and help me take her to the emergency room. I will take care of her there."

The two soldiers carried her into an elevator. Luckily enough, there were several empty wheelchairs on the side of it. Lidia DelToro was placed in one, with the doctor holding her head, as it bobbled from side to side.

Thurston said to the soldiers, "I do not know what your orders are, but I can manage from here. If you were told to stand guard at the lab, better return there. I think the doctor here was working on something top secret that needs to be protected at all cost."

The soldiers looked at each other. Evidently, their orders had been to guard the lab, not the doctor, so they saluted Dr. Thurston and returned to their post.

Thurston used his cell phone to call the guys waiting in the ambulance, speaking loud enough to be heard. "Yes, I am afraid Doctor DelToro had another one of those seizures she suffers from. Yes, we are on our way to the ER. Yes, I will meet you there. Thank you."

From the very busy Emergency Room, it was relatively simple to push DelToro's wheelchair to the exit, put her in the ambulance, and drive away.

As they were leaving, two black SUVs with Leopold and his men on board pulled in.

Chapter 20
THE ENHANCEMENT TEAM

They all converged at the apartment of General Silvia Fuentes Graham, codenamed " Tigress." Someone made the joke that the place had become an authentic zoo, as in addition to the "Tigress," there was "the Lioness," "the Moose," "The Badger," "the Wolf" and "the Rabbit." Someone else proposed giving Dr. Thurston the moniker of "Doctor Quack Quack." They debated what nickname to give to Vince Batagliari, since apparently nobody knew what animal was native to Italy.

"It is the wolf; the wolf is the official animal of Italy, but as it happens that name is taken," said Kirk White.

"He can be Wolf Two," said Moose.

Dr. Thurston, after having placed Dr. DelToro in a spare bedroom with her feet tied to the bed, and having given her an extra doses of Valium IV, returned to the room. Hearing the last part of the conversation, he said, "Why don't we ask Vincenso what animal, if any, he likes and go from there?"

"Doctor Quack-Quack is right.... Hey, Vince, what is your favorite animal?" –said Moose again.

"Well, I like cats and dogs, but I don't care what name you give me. I guess Cat is fine," said Vince.

"Cat is it then?" said General Silvia. "However, I do not like the moniker you have given to Dr. Thurston. You should show more respect to the man who has treated and coped with you for so many years now."

"As he should," Moose said. "He made us the mess we are."

"That is so unfair of you to say, Moose," said Karla, who until that moment had been sitting quietly drinking a Diet Coke while Kelly Carter was snoring loudly, sleeping on the same couch. "It was the military that made us the way we are, and I, for one, am grateful. It has been explained many times over the years that Dr. Thurston and his colleagues Colton and Pratt, developed the serum in the hope of helping, or possibly curing Alzheimer's disease and perhaps improving the cognitive abilities of some mentally retarded individuals."

"Karla is telling the truth. The serum was not supposed to make us Captain America. It simply increased our already present abilities and each one of us was chosen very carefully among hundreds of other enlisted men because they detected some special abilities. The serum simply increased those abilities," said General Fuentes.

"What Karla and Silvia have said is exactly true, in a capsule," said Dr. Thurston. "What they have omitted, or perhaps don't know, and I am going to say it again to the benefit of First Lieutenant 'Cat,' who is the newest member of the 'Enhancement Team,' is that all of you were selected first for your intelligence, valor, fearlessness, good judgment and loyalty. But also we looked into strength, dexterity, endurance and special abilities and interests. We hoped the serum would increase those.

"The serum worked as expected, but acted somewhat different in each of the subjects, especially in men vs. women. It was totally missed on several physical examinations and tests, but some had congenital problems with the heart, brain, lungs or with their genetic makeup. Others—we simply never found out why—died. That was when, despite the pressure from the military, I refused to continue the experiments."

He took a sip of coffee and continued: "Another thing that we did not know was that the serum would not only increase the good qualities of an individual but also the bad ones, especially anger, resentment, violent behavior, and the propensity to steal and even murder—the last one, which, thank God, none of you developed. And you and the Lord God know that I have tried to help you cope with your problems over the years, despite the reluctance of some of you to be treated."

Another sip of coffee. "All these years I have been working to find an antidote for the friken serum without any success. However, I have found a combination of two

116

medications used mainly for the treatment of epilepsy that works for impulse disorders, which I believe is the appropriate name for the problems you have. I think you should let me try it on you once the problems at hand are resolved."

"Or we get killed," Moose spoke up again

"Exactly, or if we get killed." It was Rabbit this time.

"Okay, men, you have listened to the doctor. Now we have to plan what are we going to do.

"First, we have to get these two sleeping beauties out of my apartment, as I do not think it is safe for any of us to keep them here. Besides Lioness needs to get back to her husband and kids.

"My husband and I own a cabin in the woods nearby in Virginia. It is isolated enough, and we can take a well-deserved vacation there. We can even take the kids with us. They would not say anything. As you may know, my husband is an ex-Marine and he loves to get into shit like this. Besides, the only one we have to worry about escaping is 'Doctor Bullfight,' and we all will keep an eye on her 24/7," said Karla.

"That is a great idea," said several members of the team.

"Okay, then, but let us wait. The senator is supposed to call me to let me know what he has scheduled for tomorrow. His aide Jason has been informed about the death of the Chinese Doctor and the extraction of 'Doctor Bullfight,'" said Silvia.

The phone rang seconds later; it was past one o'clock in the morning. It was Senator McClain

After listening to the Senator, Silvia said to the people in the room, "The Senator has arranged for a joint meeting of the two chambers of Congress, to be attended also by members of the press this morning at 10 a.m."

"McClain thinks the President and General Masters have been informed about his plan by Congresspersons loyal to him and, therefore, it would be way too dangerous to bring any of these two women to the Capitol; apparently, he just wants to play the tapes, drives, discs or whatever it is that he has and answer questions from both, Congress members, news Media and even members of the public. He expects problems, so we have to be there, in civilian attire of course".

"Okay, men, get some sleep. But first, wake up Mrs. Carter and help carry DelToro to Karla's car. Pretend to be drunk. The neighbors won't be too surprised. I throw parties here once in a while. Wrap the little girl in a blanket while she still sleeping. She goes with Karla also."

"Done, boss," said Moose. "So we are a team again?" "Yes, we are, TEAM ENHANCEMENT!"

"I would call it TEAM ZOO instead," said Vincent Batagliari.

"Zoo is better," said Wolf. "Certainly shorter.

Chapter 21
REPORT TO THE PRESIDENT

General Masters had been called by POTUS, to give a report of the day's developments. Masters had postponed the interview until he had news from Leopold. Now that he knew that those were not the kind of news the President wanted to hear, he wanted to be miles away from the White House. Yet, he had no choice but to obey, and so they were meeting late that night in the President's Private Residence living room on the third floor of the White House.

The President was definitely not happy, and Masters knew that he would become much more upset, so he decided to get it over with as fast as possible.

"No, we have not found the Carter woman. No, we do not have the scientist lady. No, we do not have the Chinese scientist either, but he would not be able to open his mouth to incriminate us because he is dead."

The President's rubicund face became red as a beet, to the point that he had to sit down, pour himself a generous amount of brandy from a decanter onto a nearby table, and swallow it in one gulp.

"So, Charlie, you are telling me that you have not been able to find a woman whose face is well-known to almost everyone in the USA and who, at the time of her disappearance, was wearing a dress so green that it probably glows in the dark."

Masters attempted to save face by responding, "That is true, sir, but neither have the Secret Service or the FBI."

"I know that, Charlie. That is because, as you are aware, I don't want to get those agencies involved in this most private matter. So I have limited them to looking for Kelly Carter and the guy who helped her get away and keeping an eye on the residences of my best-known enemies."

Charles Masters did not say it but thought to himself: "To

accomplish that, you'll need a million-man army."

"The FBI has searched the home of Senator McCain, because you said Carter may have called him, and they found nothing. As to the man who attacked the Secret Service guys and was seen running away with her, he has been identified as a homeless Ex-Army Ranger who suffers from delusions, probably due to PTSD.

"The FBI has also located the green dress. A homeless woman said that a person fitting the description of Kelly gave it to her. But, of course, neither Kelly nor First Lieutenant Vincenso Batagliari was in any place nearby."

"What did the woman who gave her the phone number of McClain to Carter had to say?"

Masters did not want to make the President angrier, so he did not tell him that she was either dead or fighting for his life. So he simply said, "She did not know anything about it. In fact, at the time of the call, she had no knowledge that Mrs. Carter had lost her mind."

"Okay then, what about the Chinese and the Spanish doctors?"

"I am afraid that something rather unhappy and unforeseen took place at the home of the Chinese doctor. And, as far as Dr. DelToro, she has not been located yet."

"What the hell do you mean by rather unhappy and unforeseen took place at the home of the Chinese doctor. Your men did not hurt him. Did they?"

Masters knew that this was coming, and that "the cleaners" that he had sent to make the corpses disappear had arrived too late, as the police and the media were already at the scene. So, he related the story that Leopold had told him.

"So, are you telling me, Charles, that your men rang the bell at the home of this Doctor to invite him to have a chat with me, and he charged at them with karate kicks and chops for no reason, and therefore they had to kill him?"

"Well, not exactly, sir. For reasons of security, my men were not briefed about you being involved on this. Therefore your name was not mentioned."

"So, Doctor Chin is dead. Was anyone else in the house?"

"I am afraid the man's wife was there and, as she took part in the melee, the men had no choice but to shoot her as well."

"Shit, shit, shit, and more shit! You fucked up big-time Masters. Do you know that the wife of the Doctor was a second cousin of the head of the Chinese Communist Party? The Chinese are not going to like this a bit. It is going to become a major international scandal. I will have to call the Chinese Premier and give him the news personally. We have to make it look like a simple home invasion that went sour."

Now Masters was scared. He knew that the Chinese were not stupid, and they would send their own undercover investigators to investigate. If they found the truth, his life would not be worth much, despite being the Chief of Staff of POTUS. He knew that Orientals are very patient, and he was not going to be Chief of Staff forever.

Neither of them knew about the Chinese couple's little daughter

Then the private cell phone of POTUS rang.

"Hello, good evening, Senator. Yes, I am glad to hear your voice. No, I was unaware of that, and I have not yet been invited. 10 a.m., you said? And the press and the public have been invited? Yes, probably fake news, false accusations. You know, Senator, our enemies are always trying to discredit us and the party. Thank you, Senator Bird. Yes, I certainly appreciate the information and your loyalty. Good night."

"What was that, sir?"

"More shit, Masters." "Senator McClain probably has all the information from Kelly Carter. I do not know how she sent it to him, but he has called for a meeting of the two chambers of Congress, with press and public present, for tomorrow at 10 a.m."

"We will have to discredit them and deny anything they say. You should call your own press conference," said Masters.

"I most certainly will, Chuck, but not before we know what they know and what are they going to say. We will call

Fox News and all other news outlets that are friendly to us.

"We also should inform the guys from the pharmaceutical companies about the shit storm that is coming and tell them to deny everything and that all the business we discussed is now on hold. At least for the time being."

"Sir, you mentioned that the public will be invited. What do you think about my contacts getting in touch with our friends, the 'Proud Boys,' 'the True Patriots,' and as many as possible of the other groups that are so loyal to you? They can get in with the public and raise hell there."

"Perhaps that is not a bad idea. However, I am sure that McClain, et al, would have their own security and surveillance. So tell them to send some of their least known and more loyal members and, of course, not to bring any weapons with them.

"However, I would not be extremely upset if someone gives someone a firearm and that someone becomes so irate about the false accusations that they are going to bring against their beloved president, that he can't control himself and tries to kill the bastards? In fact, Flynn, I would not mind at all if the someone who gets shot is that son of a bitch McClain and-or that treasonous bitch Kelly Carter."

"That can certainly be easily arranged, sir. Please let me take care of that."

"Ok, do it Flynn, but be careful, and do not fuck up again, I do not want you to spend the rest of your days in a federal prison."

Masters thought to himself: "You mean the rest of OUR DAYS in a federal prison."

"Do not worry, sir, I would not even call those guys myself. I have someone who I trust to do it, and that someone could provide a weapon to one or two of those poor stupid losers, to do their patriotic duty for us."

"Okay, get on it right away. Oh, and before I forget, since your people could not find the DelToro girl, did they at least get her computers?"

"Yes, sir, they did. Although they had some trouble at the beginning. There were two MPs guarding the laboratory and they would not let my men get in till I called the guards personally and told them to allow them to take the computers."

"Shit, another stupid lose end, I hope this one does not come back to haunt us."

"If you wish I can take care of those two MP guards Sir"

"No, no, no, we have more than enough corpses for one day. Heck, not for one day, for one year...You know that I hate violence, Chuck. Violence is your department and specialty. Mine is business. I am a businessman and, even though I understand that some degree of violence is necessary from time to time, I prefer negotiations".

"That I understand, but you have to realize that sometimes shit happens".

"And it always smells bad, Charles; shit always stinks."

Chapter 22
REPORT TO CONGRESS

Silvia got up at 5 a.m., as she usually did, despite having gone to bed very late the night before. Her military training allowed her to sleep well and get up rested. After going for her morning jog, she got on the phone and called the chief of security at the Capitol, informing him that there was going to be an unscheduled meeting of the two chambers of Congress, with the presence of the media and probably some members of the public. The matter to be disclosed was of utmost importance for national security and there might be attempt on the life of Senator James McClain, his wife or perhaps other members of Congress. She stressed the need to be on the lookout for snipers and armed individuals among the public.

The still sleepy chief of security was surprised, but he was thankful that she called early, especially since he had not yet been informed about the meeting. Again, it was only 6 in the morning, and the meeting was supposed to be at 10.

He was so sleepy that he forgot to ask who was calling. At first, he thought of going back to bed and regarded the call as a prank, but then the phone rang again. This time, it was Jason White, the senator's right hand, with confirmation of the date and time of the meeting.

The chief was no longer sleepy. He put coffee in the Keurig, bread in the toaster and started making phone calls.

At 9 a.m., Senator McClain called a taxi and got in it with Jason and Dr. Thurston. Vincenso Batagliari, Rabbit, Wolf, and Edith McClain followed in the senator's car. Silvia and Moose joined the caravan a few blocks ahead. They all headed to the US Capitol.

It was obvious that Silvia's call had been effective, as the security in front of the Capitol was more than double the usual. Officers wore bulletproof vests and carried AR-15s in addition to their side arms. They were checking all vehicles approaching. People going inside had to go through metal detectors and bomb sniffing dogs.

Admission tickets had been e-mailed by the senator's staff to members of the press and selected civilians of different party affiliations, as the senator thought that people from all walks of life had the right to be informed. Also, the event was to be televised nationally and internationally—quite a feat considering the short time they had to pull it all together.

The members of the Enhancement team were given credentials stating that they were the senator's personal security team and that they were allowed to carry concealed weapons.

The senator's entry into the Capitol was no problem, as most of the reporters waiting outside stormed the official car. He, Thurston and Jason stepped out of the taxi undetected.

Unknown to them was the fact that Leopold and five of his men had procured tickets as well and were there along with some other men loyal to General Masters. They also had special permits to carry weapons, signed by General Masters.

Only Mrs. McClain, Jason, and Vincent sat near the senator. Although he himself was not seated, he greeted every member of Congress as they entered the chamber and evidently gave brief advances of the news to be disclosed.

The rest of the team was spread among the crowd.

Silvia watched for a man with a scar on his face. She saw him immediately when he walked into the place and warned her team via her small microphone: "Scarface in the premises, next to last row, under the balcony. Believe has at least three men with him. Not together. Beware."

At ten minutes to 10, the place was full, with people standing on the balcony and sitting on the steps. So, the chairperson gave the floor to McClain after a short introduction.

McClain began. "My fellow congressmen and congresswomen, press members, fellow Americans. It is with a heavy heart that I come here today to denounce to you, to the entire country and to the whole world a crime that is beyond treason, a crime that only be compared to those committed by Nazi Germany or the Şoviet purges; a much worse crime when it was to be committed by the persons, we entrust our security, our liberty, and our democracy to."

He paused at this point as it appeared that everyone in the room had stopped breathing.

"Those persons, fellow Americans, are none less than the President, Vice-President, Chief of Staff, and a group of greedy individuals from a handful of drug companies—which you know as Big Pharma."

At this point, some of the people screamed, some said, "Shame, shame," and a few from the gallery yelled: "Liar, liar, fake news, fake news, liars, liars." These few were soon followed by others, in total, perhaps twenty of thirty, many shouting insults:

"Fucking liars!" "Pieces of shit!" "Communists!" "Assholes," etc., etc.

Silvia observed the scar-faced man who, although he was not shouting insults, made a sign with his head to a redheaded guy who was about ten feet away from him. She saw that the man reached into the back of his trousers to pull a gun.

Silvia was too far away from the man, and the place was too crowded to do anything without hurting some innocent bystander, so she said on her microphone, "Man with a gun at 3 o'clock next to the fat guy with a red shirt."

Wolf saw that the guy—who by then had a gun in his hand, shouting, "Liar son of a bitch, I am going to fucken kill you"—was pointing at the Senator, who was at least thirty feet away.

Wolf thought, either this guy is an exceedingly good shooter or a perfect idiot. Wolf did not wait to find out. He drew the knife he had in his boot and threw it at the guy, aiming at his neck in case he was wearing a bulletproof vest. The knife hit the target with deadly accuracy, with the knife going from Adam's apple to the cervical spine. He was dead before hitting the floor, but he still fired the gun as he fell.

The bullet hit the ceiling, and no one was hurt.

Of course, there was a great pandemonium, with people

yelling and crouching on the floor. Many ran out of the place, tripping on each other, and some got hurt as they fell and got trampled. Most ran as fast as they could, but many stayed after the order was restored and the public was led out of the place.

The paramedics rushed to the help of the man hit by Wolfe's knife, who, by then, was nothing but a corpse. So, they assisted those who fell or got trampled. Fortunately, no one was seriously hurt. The Capitol Police made some arrests of guys and gals suspected to be connected with the shooter. Most were later released.

Scarface and his men left in the confusion, and Wolf followed them.

All the media people, although scared, stayed put, and all of the congresspersons stayed as well.

The meeting resumed an hour later without the public present, but Americans were informed that it would be televised later across the nation in its entirety.

Senator McClain continued his eloquent speech. He described the all too convenient "accidental" deaths of Dr. Christian Shaw and General William Bright—the only two persons who refused to play the game that the President and his friends proposed—the murders of Dr. Chin-Ghan-Do and his wife, plus the attack on Mrs. Laura Mason, the woman who provided the Senator's phone number to Kelly Carter. He played the tapes recorded by the latter, showed the video of her telling her story and also played the recording of the conversation between Dr. Thurston and Dr. DelToro, the previous night. The senator was careful not to accuse POTUS, directly or by name, of any involvement in those murders, but his guilt was implied.

The senator had Vincenso Batagliari and Dr. Thurston confirm the story. Thurston added that, if it had not been for the heroic intervention of First Army Lieutenant Batagliari, Mrs. Carter would likely be now dead or confined to a mental asylum.

They stated that Mrs. Carter and DelToro would be willing to testify before Congress when requested, but they were not present today, as they feared for their lives. "Justifiably so, considering the events that just took place in this chamber few minutes ago."

There was a clamor in the room, followed by a strong call from members of both political parties for the immediate impeachment of the President and Vice-President, their prosecution after that, and the indictment of all those involved in the plot.

Of course, there were those diehards who questioned the evidence presented on the videotape of Kelly Carter telling her story, especially her recording of the conversation from the Oval Office.

The conversation between Dr. Thurston and Dr. DelToro, whom he recorded, was also played, and questions were asked if it was recorded with the knowledge and consent of Dr. DelToro. Otherwise, it may not have legal validity.

Dr. Thurston knew that but, of course, dodged the question. McClain, who was a lawyer by profession, had told him that the legal validity of that recording would be questioned. Yet, all congressmen present, and the members of the press had heard it, and there was no way to erase it from their brains.

In the end, the consensus was that the Chamber of Representatives would meet that same afternoon to consider the impeachment, and if they reached an agreement, the Senate would meet as soon as the following day to vote on the same issue.

At the time, it was almost inevitable that most of both chambers would approve the resolution.

The diehard POTUS congresspersons got out of the chambers and on their cell phones to report to the White House. However, they were mostly, and above all, concerned about their political survival.

Chapter 23
THE VICE-PRESIDENT

He was a meek-looking guy, short, bald, spectacled, slightly chubby, shy, and introverted, a man of few words and a fanatic follower of POTUS, to the point that—if the President had asked him to kiss his ass—he literally would have done it.

However, Joe Whurty was a lawyer by profession and was not a stupid person.

The three of them, the president and the president, plus General Masters, were in the Oval Office after the President had given his own press conference, only hours after the events at the Capitol and, of course, denied all the accusations while vilifying Kelly Carter and Senator McClain.

He had been cautious at discrediting Vince Batagliari because he was a decorated veteran and member of a well-known and respected military family. He had had no praise for him either, labeling him as a deranged Veteran who suffered from delusions due to posttraumatic stress disorder and who had been easily manipulated by a treacherous woman—also suffering from mental problems and delusions—along with an ambitious politician who was taking advantage of both of these mentally infirm individuals. He had labeled the charges and accusations "ridiculous, baseless and fake," knowing well that the media did not buy his defense and knowing well that his accusers had strong evidence against him.

The Vice-President spoke, mostly addressing his boss, "I know, sir, that you realize this is a very serious problem we need to be realistic. Only three Presidents in the history of the United States have been impeached: Andrew Johnson, Bill Clinton and Donald Trump—the latter twice. None of them were confirmed by the Senate and, therefore, none was removed from Office. Richard Nixon probably would have been impeached and removed, but he resigned before that happened."

"Where are you going with that Joe; are you trying to scare the President?" interrupted Masters in the usual commanding manner he used when he addressed those he considered inferior to him

"No, General. I am simply trying to be realistic and prepare the President, and you, and yes, myself for the storm that is breaking in our doors."

"Go on, Joe," said the President.

"McClain and the rest of our foes are not stupid. He is a seasoned politician and a good lawyer, and he knew that going public was the best way to protect his hide and that of his witnesses.

"Also, he is preventing you from using the FBI or any other federal agency against them. In fact, the FBI will probably start investigating us and they will likely turn Kelly, Dr. DelToro, the Italian lieutenant, and whoever else they have as witnesses to the protection to the FBI.

"They will ask Congress to name a Special Prosecutor, and we will very likely be impeached at this time. I would doubt very much that the Senate would not vote for impeachment. What we are being accused of is much worse than what Nixon did.

"I think the representatives will come up with an impeachment vote in a matter of days, perhaps hours, because, as we well know we do not hold the majority there and they hate our guts. The Senate is ours and, even if it wasn't, they take much longer to get things done. They will want to play and replay the tapes. They will interrogate the witness over and over and, more than anything, they will evaluate what result their vote would have in their political futures.

"Therefore, we have some time to prepare our defense and even to walk away with several million in our pockets."

Both POTUS and Masters ask at once: "How?"

The Vice-Pres continued: "You have a very large group of very loyal, almost fanatic, and I would dare to say, stupid followers and another group-albeit smaller but very important: a group of rich followers. And let us not forget our partners in crime: Big Pharma. Offer them full executive pardon in exchange for generous donations of several million dollars.

"Of course, we are going to place all the blame on them—greedy corporate sons of bitches—who came to us to propose a deal that could make us billions for our country through selling a vaccine that would prevent a deathly virus from killing millions of people around the world—without telling us they will be actually the ones releasing the virus with the cooperation of some scientists in China"

"But that is not the truth, Joe," said the President.

"Of course it is not true, sir. Since when has a good politician told the truth? But that is what we are going to tell Congress and the media.

"We tell them that the scientists who developed the virus also tried to convince us about their theory that releasing that virus would benefit mankind by reducing poverty worldwide by sterilizing large masses of the population and, at the same time, saving governments trillions of dollars by reducing the number of government-dependent people."

"I bet many people will like that idea," said Masters.

"All that sounded very good," said the President, "and to this day, I agree with Dr. DelToro's theory. I never understood why those religious groups that oppose abortion also oppose birth control. If there is no pregnancy, there is no need for abortion. I do not know what part of that those people don't understand."

"That is totally fucking moronic," said General Masters.

Ignoring General Master's remarks, the Vice-President continued, "I agree with you 200%, sir, but saying that publicly would be unacceptable and likely politically suicidal. So we should be very careful at not expressing our opinions out of this room.

"We can use social media to reach the first group of your fans—of course not using our names or accounts—and also encourage them to start demonstrations in our favor all over the country, but especially here in D.C. while also soliciting monetary donations for our defense fund. Thousands, if not millions, of donations of five, ten, or a hundred bucks soon add up to sizable amounts of money. That would be in addition to what money we can get from other big donors besides our partners from Big Pharma. I am willing to bet that we can raise at least a hundred million in less than a month."

"You are a genius, Joe. I know I was not wrong to pick you as my running mate. But, of course, I am never wrong."

"It sounds too good to be true," said Masters, ignoring the boasting to which he had become accustomed.

"Joe's ideas are certainly worth a shot," said POTUS.

"One more thing, sir," said the Vice President.

"What is it?" asked Masters, who was mortified that the President had actually considered the proposition coming out of this little man's mouth.

"It concerns you, General. We can be impeached for considering the proposal of the CEOs of Big Pharma. But there are deaths involved. It is not too farfetched that, after the impeachment, we could be charged with murder, or at least with being accessory to murder and sent to prison"

Joe Whurty paused to see the effect his words had caused on Masters, a guy he disliked to the point of hatred, perhaps out of jealousy due to his favor with the President.

Then he continued: "Now, since you, General, have been in charge of the murder department, whoever you hired or used to commit those deeds needs to be—what is the word you military people use? Neutralized...is that it?

"Oh, and better if it is done fast before the Chinese get to those whoever people. Because, as it happens, the scientist that was murdered was highly regarded by his government and his wife happened to be a cousin of the Communist Party leader. I am sure you have seen movies about how the Orientals always get the information they want from their prisoners. But again, you may have used those techniques yourself on the Muslims in Afghanistan."

Masters was now very pissed off and really wanted to punch the little man right in the middle of his smirking mouth, but it appeared that the President was amused and believing every word that the VP was saying. So, it appeared to General Masters that Joe Whurty was now among the President's favorites, so he simply replied: "I am not concerned. China is far away and I am the Chief of Staff of the President of the United States."

"Unfortunately for you General, if the events here in Washington evolve as I predicted, we will all be out of the job soon. The Chinese likely will send a big delegation to claim the bodies of Dr. Chin-Ghan and his wife. I understand there is an orphaned little girl that some relative probably will claim. I am afraid that we will have no control of who will be coming among those in the Chinese delegation."

Masters suddenly felt diminished by this small, shy person he had obviously underestimated, who now toyed with him and his fears. A chill ran down his spine when he considered that he could be "neutralized" as well, and perhaps not only by the Chinese.

One thing was clear, and the VP had it right: Leopold and those who helped him had to be neutralized. After all, he was still a general in the United States Army. Although he retired a couple of years before becoming Chief of Staff, he hoped to still have command over some special force unit that had fought with him in the Middle East and had now become semi-legal businessmen. He recalled that those men liked money above all else, and he had access to money, not only his own but that of the President.

He would deal with this little man some other time.

Chapter 24
SCANDAL

The front page of most newspapers in the USA and abroad, read as follows:
"THE PRESIDENT OF THE UNITED STATES IS ACCUSED OF HIGH TREASON, ATTEMPTED GENOCIDE, POSSIBLE MURDER OR ACCESSORY TO MURDER, AND COLLUSION WITH A FOREIGN COUNTRY TO DO HARM TO THE CITIZEN OF THE UNITED STATES OF AMERICA."

And

"THE PRESIDENT EMPHATICALLY DENIES ALL CHARGES, CALLS THEM FAKE NEWS AND BELIEVES IT IS PART OF A POLITICAL PLOY TO REMOVE HIM FROM THE PRESIDENCY"

The radio and televised media did not stay behind. All went on to describe the events at the Capitol and gave little or no credence to what the President said at the press conference that followed those events. A handful of newspaper journalists and conspiracy theorists' radio hosts defended him, and a television network known for its loyalty to POTUS, although not siding openly with the president, just asked the public to be patient and wait until all the facts were known and all the witnesses were heard.

As predicted by the Vice-President, the FBI and Homeland Security took over the protection of all the witnesses, and Congress called for a special prosecutor to be nominated as soon as possible. The House of Representatives called a special session the morning after the events at the Capitol, to draw the articles of impeachment.

Social media went crazy, with most people asking for the immediate removal of POTUS without waiting for Congress to impeach him and inviting people to come out to demonstrate in the streets to demand his removal. And out they went, from Seattle to Tallahassee and from Juneau to Phoenix, people came out.

From both sides POTUS supporters—especially from rural America and the Bible Belt, but also in major urban cities—enticed by the messages received on social media, came to demonstrate and ask that those who wanted to depose the President be jailed or hanged because they considered them traitors.

There were frequent clashes between the two groups. There was violence, there was arson, there was looting from both sides and from those who were there just for the thrill and the looting and who did not give shit for one side or another. And there were multiple casualties, both among demonstrators and anti-riot police. In some cities, entire neighborhoods were lit a fire. Gradually, over several days, the groups supporting the President became smaller and the ones requesting his dismissal became larger, but not until the two groups separately converged on Washington DC.

Thank God the Police were ready, and the major had activated the National Guard, so there was less damage than in other cities, with the exception of casualties, which were multiple as people on both sides carried firearms and used them. Often times the National Guard or the police had no choice but to return fire.

It lasted almost three days.

In the aftermath, there were over fifty casualties, twenty of them dead, including two National Guardsmen and one police officer.

More than three hundred people were arrested. Of course, these disturbances delayed the House of Representatives meeting by four days, as it was not safe to travel the streets of the capital during the riots.

This delay was much to the delight of the White House, which at the time issued several executive pardons and collected millions of dollars in donations.

The White House played the role of the good guys by calling the fighting factions to stop and return home, while at the same time, they were hoping that they didn't.

Chapter 25
WOLF

The Zoo team, as Vince preferred to call them, was meeting at the cabin of Karla Messer (code name Lioness). Her husband had left with their two kids, and they were awaiting a call from Senator McClain to tell them if they had to surrender the key witness to the FBI and, if so, when and where.

Dr. Thurston was present not only to give opinions and help make plans but also to administer sedatives to Dr. DelToro as she had turned violent. On the two occasions when she awoke, she tried to bite Karla, forcing her to tie her up and put a muzzle on her mouth.

Wolf was the last one to arrive.

As soon as he showed up, they greeted him and congratulated him on what he had done earlier at the Capitol, probably saving not only McClain but several other lives.

"Just a lucky shot," Wolf said. "I have other news. Not only do I have the picture of Scarface on my cell, but I know where he is hiding. I had to borrow someone's motorcycle and I followed him when he left the capitol this morning. He is in a warehouse that is supposed to be a car repair shop."

"Good job, pal," said Moose. "General Fuentes has his picture on her cell too."

General Fuentes said, "I sent his picture to Army Intelligence and we got a hit almost immediately. His name is Leopold Mishanivich, a Russian defector from the KGB. He switched sides in Afghanistan and was brought to this country…guess by whom?"

"Let me guess," said Dr. Thurston, "Your colleague, General Charles Flynn Masters."

"Bingo. He brought Leopold to the US because he promised to reveal important information about the Russians. It turned out he did not give us anything important or anything that we did not know already, but somehow he managed to stay and become a US citizen.

"He did not have the scar back then. Apparently he got that trying to escape from a fire. He had to jump through a window and cut his face, plus he had some serious burns on his back"

"Through the years he has done some dirty work for Masters and others. Plus he is very likely dealing with stolen vehicles and is suspected to have connections with the Mexican drug cartels. And he may be a rapist"

"I think he tried to rape Laura Masson. We just got there on time," said Dr. Thurston.

"There is more," said Silvia Fuentes.

"Dr. Thurston, please guess where that fire happened?"

"No idea, Silvia... Where?"

"At The Laboratory of Dr. Bruce Colton and Dr. Neil Pratt."

"Shit...do you think that they gave this guy the serum?"

"I have no idea, Doctor. They were your friends, and that is your area of expertise."

"Well, Bruce and Neil were pretty frustrated when we stopped administering the serum and I destroyed all remaining vials. In fact, that was the reason that we became distant after being close friends for years. They wanted to continue experimenting by treating the mentally retarded and Alzheimer's patients, but without government funding, there was no money for that. I know that they approached Lederle and other labs without finding anybody interested. Everyone knew about the deaths from the serum. So they may have tried to treat private patients for a fee. Our friend Leopold could have been one of them. Who knows? Both of them are dead now.

"I believe it will be best to assume that this fellow, Leopold, was injected with the serum. They gave three doses to each one of us, so let us also assume that this fellow Leopold got at least one dose before the fire broke out. Witnesses at the time claimed that there was a lot of shouting and sounds of things breaking before the fire started, and the third body that was found later in what was left of the lab had traces in his blood of what the coroner called 'an unknown substance'. That person, whoever he was, was blamed for starting the fire."

"Okay, men. There is that possibility, and we have to be aware of it. However, if Leopold—who definitely attacked Mrs. Mason and likely killed Doctor Chin-Ghan-Do and his wife, and perhaps also had some role in the "accident" that killed the two fellows who did not go along with POTUS and his plan—is working for General Masters, he is a valuable asset we could use to get Masters, POTUS, and the Vice-Pres. Therefore our goal would be to capture him and force to confess," said General Fuentes.

"If I were Masters, I would not like a fellow who did my dirty work to be walking around free of care. Leopold is too dangerous for then, and they likely will have him terminated," said Wolf

"I agree with Wolf. We have to scare Leopold into testifying against them in order to save his skin. I will have someone other than us deliver a note to Leopold warning him and asking him to meet me at a public place to discuss the issue of his protection."

"However, are you guys sure that the cops are not looking for me after the Capitol thing?" Wolf said.

"Sure, as sure as can be. We are not sure, but according to the media and social networks you are hailed as a hero," said Karla and asked the General, "Silvia, have you shown the picture of this guy Leopold to the little girl, Lia? She may have seen the face of the guy who killed her parents, or you think it would be too traumatic for her?" The question was not directed to anyone in particular, and as there was no answer, she continued:

"Lia is a brave little girl, and although she has been crying from time to time, she played with my kids, and they had a few laughs. We can ask her first if she saw the faces of the intruders and if she says yes, we can ask her if we show her a picture, she is able to recognize the person."

"Yes, I suppose that we can do that, but I do not want to

turn her to the FBI. She has had more trauma in one day than most grownup people can have in a lifetime," said Silvia.

"We have noticed that you two have bonded very well, and I do not blame you, Silvia. Lia is such a beautiful and charming little girl, straightforward to get attached to her. But remember that she probably has family in China, and someone will come to claim her," said Dr. Thurston.

"I know and it is too bad. I would not mind keeping her."

"Neither would I," said Karl. "But what it is it is."

"Okay, ladies, we agree the kid is adorable, but we have bigger problems at hand. Do we still have to protect the senator and his family, or do we help to obtain more evidence against POTUS and his clan?" asked Wolf.

General Silvia Fuentes Graham, as the leader of the pack answered:

"I do not think that we have to be concerned about the security of the senator. He has Jason, plus he is protected now by the FBI and Homeland Security. I doubt that anyone would try anything against him. He was extremely clever in going public with this scandal."

"What about the mobs? I have seen a lot of people arriving to DC, and more and more people are also gathering around the Capitol and the White House. Most seem to be critics of the administration. But, while coming here, I have seen, some placards and banners supporting him"? said Vince.

"That could be indeed concerning, but I believe that the senator is neither at the Capitol, nor at his residence at the moment, and I am sure that the major is going to deploy the National Guard," said the General, and continued:

"Let us go ahead with Wolf's plan. Have someone deliver a note to Leopold. See if he is willing to meet with us. Then see if he can convince him that we are his only hope to come out of this alive if is willing to testify. Meanwhile we keep twenty-four-hour surveillance on his place and prepare to use alternative methods to extract him if he refuses our offer."

"The note has to be brief, scary, and to the point," said Rabbit. "How about simply: 'Masters is planning to kill you.

Best get out of there fast. If you want protection, meet me at the Lincoln Memorial at 18:30. Come alone.'"

Although it was not required because General Silvia Fuentes-Graham was the leader and decision-maker, they unanimously agreed that the message was perfect. Once it was written, Wolf was to deliver it accompanied by Rabbit, who was charged with installing surveillance equipment to monitor the activities of the people in Leopold's garage.

t that time, General Silvia's cell phone rang, and she answered, announcing to the group, "It is the Senator. The FBI is ready to pick up the witness. I do not think that they should know about this place. Where do you fellows think will be a good place to do the exchange?"

"How about our martial arts school? We had no classes today due to the events in DC. I can do it by myself. You guys can follow from a distance, but first, let me have a few minutes with Lia concerning the picture of the murderer also. Dr. Thurston, can you check on the DelToro woman and perhaps give her a bit more sedation. She has been rather rude and rowdy when awake. I have been trying to be nice to her, even helped her to change after she peed on herself. But after that, she tried to bite me," Karla, aka the Lioness, said and left the room, followed by Thurston.

"Okay, Karla, we will do the exchange at your school." I will inform the senator and give him the address. She will ride with the Bullfighter woman and with you, Kelly, in the back, Dr. Thurston will drive with Lia riding shotgun. We will follow in two cars, a short distance behind. Let's get ready, men."

Dr. Thurston returned first and reported that Dr. DelToro was still somewhat drowsy. However, because of her reported behavior and to prevent her from jumping out of the car or becoming combative and causing an accident, he gave her another 10 mgs of Valium IV.

Karla's return took a bit longer, but when she came back, she reported that it would not be necessary to show the little girl the picture of the killer of his parents because she did not see him. She was upstairs in her room, and her mother kept yelling to her, in Chinese, to get in the closet and not to leave her room. She did not come out until she heard a female voice...Silvia's.

"A slight change of plans. The little girl will ride with me. We still follow Karla and Thurston park a block from the school. Then either the Doctor or Karla comes out and fetches the girl".

They all smiled but did not say anything. Obviously, Silvia had become concerned about the possibility that DelToro would become combative and cause an accident, in which case the little one could be hurt.

Then all got ready to leave.

Moose carried the sedated body of Doctor Lidia DelToro to the car.

Chapter 26
THE WOLF AND THE RABBIT

The Wolf and the Rabbit drove by the automobile repair shop where Leopold was suspected of being. They drove twice, ten minutes apart and in different directions in order not to raise suspicion. They did not see Leopold or any of the guys who had been at the Capitol earlier, but there was definitely some activity inside the shop. They parked the vehicle about a block away from the place and waited.

"What are we waiting for?" asked Rabbit

"We are waiting for some kid or a person who appears to need money to deliver the note to the shop," his friend responded.

"And why would someone do that, Wolf?"

"We pay them. We give him or her ten dollars."

"You have ten dollars, Wolf? I was under the impression that we all were totally broke."

"We are. Actually, we were, but the Doctor gave me one hundred bucks for expenses."

"You have a hundred bucks on you? Heck, give me that ten dollars and I will deliver the note. None of those guys know me anyway. Better give me twenty dollars and I'll also take a quick look at the inside of the shop."

"That is probably not a good idea Rabbit. What if someone recognizes you?"

"Recognize me as what? the guy who works at the computer store? Come on, man, cough up those twenty bucks."

"I guess it will be okay, but be careful. I will be watching you with the binoculars. Do not return to the car, keep walking, go around the block and I will pick you up once they cannot see you from the shop."

"Okay, okay… I will leave my gun with you because, if those guys are professionals, they can spot those who are carrying a concealed without searching the guy."

Without any more talking, Leroy Smith, the Rabbit, grabbed his twenty dollars, got out of the car and started walking towards the shop.

Wolf saw him going inside the shop. And about fifteen minutes later, just when Wolf was ready to go, pistols in hand into the shop. Rabbit emerged from the place, happy and waving goodbye to someone inside. Then, he started walking in the opposite direction of the car, in which Wolf was waiting for him.

When they finally met, Rabbit got into the car and said, "I think I deserve at least thirty bucks more. Those guys in there are really nice and have nice cars also. I was looking at a Mustang Shelby. Really neat. I think it is stolen, though, because they were a little defensive when I was looking at it. I did not see Leopold, but they did take the note. I told them the truth, that some ugly guy, whom I had never seen before, paid me ten bucks to deliver the note, as I was walking down the street looking for the address of a girl that I met this morning at the Metro."

"And they bought all that shit?"

"Every bit of it. By the way, I was able to place three micro-cameras inside when I was there, Therefore I think I deserved at least thirty bucks more."

"Rabbit, I am not sure if the Doctor gave me this money to spend it all. It was supposed to be for expenses, and, so far we've had none"

"I bet he did not say that he wants some change back. I think fifty bucks is more than a reasonable price for the beautiful performance and job I just did."

"Yes, you did a good job, pal, so what the heck. Here are the other thirty dollars. I hope the general or that senator pays us better when we are done."

"Oh, now we are mercenaries. I thought all the time that we were only doing our patriotic duty."

"That too, although there is more money in the mercenary business. I knew a guy who, after leaving the service, joined a security company that contracts with foreign governments and corporations. He has been making close to two hundred grand a year, plus benefits, including medical and dental."

"Shit, no question that we are in the wrong side of the business."

"Neither one of us, members of the Zoo team—except for the women—can expect to be hired by anyone in a legal business."

"Certainly not Badger, who escaped from jail. Or you and Moose, who were in the stockade. I was lucky to find employment on a computer shop, making just a bit over the minimum. And I think that that fellow Vincent—we code-named him Cat—also has a rap sheet as long as my arm. He is living in the streets, like I was for a while."

"Maybe we can become free agents once this shit is over. I think we can make an awesome team."

"I thought that we may be too old and a little rusty, but after I saw you throwing that knife this morning, I think we still got it."

"I hope so, pal. I hope so. Let's call the General and tell her that they can start monitoring the cameras. We have two hours before the meeting with Leopold, and I am hungry. Let's go eat something."

"You think he will show up?"

"My guess is as good as yours. But I believe he will, out of curiosity … and probably to kill the sender of the note."

Chapter 27
THE LINCOLN MEMORIAL

There were not many people at the Lincoln Memorial, as most were gathering in front of the White House and the Capitol. Plus, most of the Capital's residents were well aware of the signs of trouble brewing in the city and stayed home.

The Zoo Team arrived early, at 6 PM, in different vehicles and scattered around separately, acting like tourists or demonstrators who still wanted to visit the city's historical landmarks.

Wolf arrived at 5 minutes before 6:30 (that is 18:30 hours military time). There was still plenty of light, and it would not get dark for at least a couple more hours.

Leopold was nowhere to be seen, but the team realized that anyone wandering around could be part of his gang.

Leopold showed up at 6:35 wearing dark glasses, a cowboy hat, a T-shirt and blue jeans. Wolf could detect a pistol hidden under the shirt, tucked in the back of his belt. About six other guys arrived separately but at the same time and stayed no more than twenty feet from Leopold. He looked around, searching for the person who had sent the note.

"These guys are so blatantly obvious, I guess Leopold forgot everything he learned at the KGB School, or maybe he never learned the lessons well," Wolf thought as he scanned the area. He felt better when he located all members of his team. They all were there, even Silvia and Karla. Even Karla's husband was there. All were taking positions not close but behind each one of the presumed minions of Leopold. The only one absent was Rabbit, who had stayed behind, monitoring the cameras he had placed at Leopold's auto shop and was ready to transmit anything of importance to the team's cellular phones.

Leopold looked at his wristwatch for the fourth or fifth time and Wolf considered it was time to engage.

"Mr. Mishanivich, I presume," Wolf said

Leopold turned around like a wounded snake and put his hand to his back where he had his weapon.

Wolf calmly said, "Relax, Leopold, relax. We are just here to talk about saving your hide from your boss, General Masters."

"Who are you...? I know you. I have seen you. You are the guy who threw the knife at a man's throat this morning at the Capitol."

"Correctamundo, Leo. I see you are good at remembering faces."

"What do you want from me? Why did you send a note asking to meet here?

"Well, Leo, as it happens, we are quite certain that your boss, General Charles Flynn Masters, is planning to erase your face, as well as the rest of you, from the world of the living. In other words, he is planning to fucken kill you."

"I do not know any General Masters and I would not know why he would want to kill me."

"Okay, if you want to play dumb that is fine with me, Leo. But you have to do better or the KGB will be ashamed of how poorly one of its trainees is doing in the lying department. By the way, is it okay if I call you Leo? Leopold is an ugly name."

"No, you cannot call me Leo, but you can try to call me sir. And what about KGB? I do not know anything about KGB. Isn't that like the Russian CIA?"

"We know everything about you, Leo. But if you want to cut the crap, I will explain the situation in detail to you. The residents of the White House are in really, really deep shit because, as you may or may not know, they were planning to make tons of money by simply killing a few million people in this country and around the world. Unfortunately for them a member of their own team recorded their conversation and it was made public. Before that happened, they tried to cover it up and in the process a few people were murdered, not by POTUS or the VICE PRES, not even by The Chief Of Staff, General Masters, because, obviously they could not use people from the FBI, the CIA or any other federal agency that does covert work. Therefore they needed an outsider to do the job. And that is when you came into the picture, Leo.

"Unfortunately for you, now that the shit has hit the fan, those guys will be impeached and likely prosecuted thereafter. However, the murder or the conspiracy to commit murder charges would carry more severe penalties, probably life in prison.

"Now, Mr. Ex-KGB, who do you think that the only person who can link them to those murders will be allowed to walk free and happy into the sunset? I'd guess not. You, Leopold Mishanivich, you are the one and only who can tell who sent you to kill all those people, and that is the reason why they will have you killed. I do not think that you are the only assassin that Masters can hire to do his dirty work. I think you are well aware of that, Leo, and that is why you came here tonight."

Wolf kept calling him Leo, well aware that the guy hated to be called by that name, but he had pleasure in irritating him, as he knew angry people do stupid things

However, Leopold maintained his composure and even forced a smile while responding

"You are crazy, man, whoever you are—and you are a crazy son of a bitch. Why are you telling me those things; do I look to you like a guy who can talk to the President or members of his staff?"

"The reason I am telling you all this is not because I like you, Leo, in fact, I will be very happy to kill you if Masters does not kill you first, and I am sure that the world would be a better place without you in it. However, my partners think that you are valuable to them alive and breathing, Therefore we are willing to offer you protection, if you come with us and give us testimony against Masters."

"I told you before that I do not know General Masters, I do not work for him now, and I did not work for him before or ever."

"Fucken liar, pants on fire, you are going to deny the man that extracted you from Afghanistan, brought you to this

147

country, and arranged for you to become US citizen? That is low, even for a rat like you."

"I have enough of your craziness and your insults. I am walking out of here and you better stay out of my way"

"I am afraid that that would not be possible, Leo. You see, my orders were to talk you into coming with me but if you refused, I have to use less pleasant methods to bring you in"

At this, Leopold tried to reach for his gun, a move that Wolf had anticipated. And before Leo had an opportunity to point it at Wolf, he had hit him in the forearm with the butt of his gun. The cracking of one, or perhaps both of the bones, of Leopold's forearm resounded in the shrine of the Lincoln Memorial. He cried in pain as he dropped the gun.

Leopold's men had been observing the scene from a short distance, and they came to the aid of his boss, guns in hand, only to be met by the members of the Zoo team who, seemed to arrive out of nowhere, had their own weapons pointed at each one of them.

They dropped their guns being picked up by the team who released all the clips and bullets in the pistol loading chambers dropping them back again at the feet of Leopold's men as Badger told them, "Keep your weapons guys, you are going to need them. Hopefully, you have extra clips".

Then Moose picked up the moaning Leopold with apparent no effort and carried him to one of the cars.

The few bystanders ran for cover or laid down on the floor, but as no bullets were shot and the people with the weapons were leaving, they just stood there with curiosity.

Wolf said to them as he walked away: "These Presidential supporters are crazy; imagine pulling weapons in a place like this. Nothing is sacred anymore. Thank God, we FBI people were forewarned about them, domestic terrorists."

Chapter 28
THE SHOOT OUT

The team returned to Karla's cabin in the woods and summoned Dr. Thurston to attend to Leopold's broken arm.

The Doctor arrived an hour later and administered a shot of morphine IV to the patient while attempting to set the fractured bones of Leopold's arm the best he could. As he said that, in the first place, he was not an orthopedic surgeon and, second, did not have X-rays to see how bad the fracture was or the alignment of the bones after he settled them. So, he did the best he could and put a cast on Leopold's forearm, while advising him to see a specialist as soon as possible.

Karla asked the doctor if it was possible to determine if Leopold had been injected with the enhancement serum. Dr. Thurston responded that, although the serum itself would be undetectable, his cells may show some changes suggesting enhancement. So, yes, he could draw blood, take it to the laboratory, look at the cells under the microscope, and perhaps would be able to tell one way or another. However, it would be unethical for him to draw blood without the patient's consent.

Hearing this, Badger got a syringe from the doctor's bag and inserted the needle, quite skillfully, into a vein of the still sleeping Leopold, handing it to Dr. Thurston.

"Would this be enough blood, Doc?" he asked.

"I believe so, Badger, thank you," the Doctor responded.

Leopold did not feel a thing; he was sound asleep and snoring at that time.

Rabbit called everyone to look at the screen from where he was monitoring Leopold's auto repair shop. They saw a group of men carrying heavy arms, dressed in black, and with the FBI letters on the backs of their jackets storming the shop.

The cameras showed that there were only two men at the shop and they offered no resistance. Although the sound transmitted from the cameras was very poor, they could hear the guy who appeared to be their leader asking the two guys in the shop for the whereabouts of Leopold. He forced them to kneel and put guns to the back of their heads. Since probably he did not get a satisfactory answer to his question, he shot both.

"Dear Jesus, that is bloody murder. Those guys are not FBI. They are probably General Master's goons. Looks like they are not in a hurry to leave, probably waiting for Leopold to show up," –said Vincenso, and all agreed.

"We need to warn the rest of Leopold's men. They will likely be slaughtered if they show up there. Give Leopold his cell phone and have him give them a warning call. I know they are bad guys and probably deserve what is coming to them, but at least we have to give them a chance to fight back," said Karla.

"No, can do. Unfortunately, this guy Leopold is out cold after the medications that the doctor gave him," said Badger.

"Let me see if I can unlock his phone and call them," said Rabbit as he started to push buttons on Leopold's cell phone.

As Rabbit was working on the phone, two black SUVs pulled up in front of the car repair shop and several men started to get out.

"It seems that we are too late, guys. Those fellows be sitting ducks," said Vince.

"Wait a minute, I think I have it, but they don't answer the dammed phone," said Rabbit.

"Try sending a text message," said Dr. Thurston.

"I hope it is not too late," said Rabbit.

The camera showed the first two men getting into the shop and being shot point blank with a pistol or rifle equipped with a silencer, but the other five hesitated before entering and pulled their guns out. Evidently, the text message or the voice message had gotten to them.

The camera did not pick that up, but it did show half of the men crouching behind their cars while the other half were out of view, likely trying to go to the back of the building.

These guys were not amateurs either, probably ex-KGB or

Russian army. So they would likely give those fake FBI murderers a run for their money. Nevertheless, Rabbit called 911 for the police as they all kept watching the screen.

The Russians—or whoever they were—had inferior weapons and were possibly outnumbered. However, the fake FBI guys had lost the element of surprise. Now they were the surprised ones, as they did not expect any resistance

The camera showed two of Leopold's guys coming from the rear of the building and, with two shots apiece, they killed two of the invaders who were totally taken by surprise as they did not expect an attack from the back.

Once the Russians got into the shop, they made their way to an old rusty Mercedes. Opening the trunk, they produced two AK-47s, the actual Kalashnikov rifle, and started spreading bullets all over the place, forcing the FBI guys to turn around and face them, allowing a break for the guys in the street to get inside and peg two more guys.

Then everything stopped, and both groups of people scrambled out of the shop and into their vehicles. Still, on the way out, one man in each group received a bullet and was carried away by their comrades.

"I bet the cops are coming; that is why they are running," said Rabbit.

"That was a great shootout. Better than most movies."

The police arrived in several patrol cars, but by then, everyone who was alive was already gone.

The incident was later reported as a confrontation between members of two drug cartels.

"I think that I saved some lives today," said Rabbit proudly.

"You did, indeed, and in the process, some bad dudes abandoned the world of the living," said Karla.

"Hope one balances the other," said Rabbit.

"Also gives us good leverage with our friend Leopold," said Karla again.

Chapter 29
A DEAL WITH THE DEVIL

"Hey, Doc! Can you give this guy something less strong for his pain? We need him alert and awake. You know that time is of the essence. and every time I look at him and think of what he did to the parents of that sweet girl, it makes me feel like putting a bullet right between his eyes," said Karla.

"I had to give him morphine IV in order to set the broken bones on his arm. The effect should last about four hours. Thereafter we will give him Advil or Tylenol. If he had the enhancement serum, the effect of the medication will wear off faster," said Thurston.

"We may have to break the other arm if he does not cooperate," said Moose.

"We may not have to resort to violence, fellows. I think once we show him the video of the shootout at his garage, he will be more than willing to cooperate," Rabbit said.

"Let's hope you are right, Leroy. And speaking of the enhancement serum, when are you going to get the results of the test on his blood?" said Badger.

"Yeah, and when are you going to tell us how to get back to normal again?" asked Vince.

"Whoa, whoa fellows! One question at the time. First the answer to the first one. I just drew the blood from this guy. I have the vial in my pocket. I have to take it to the lab and look at the cells under the microscope for slight changes and then run a simple chemical test to confirm or negate the finding. As to the second question, I am afraid that you guys have had irreversible changes in all the cells in your bodies and those changes are there to stay.

"However, you can learn to control your temper and other bad behavior by doing group therapy. Plus I think that very small doses of Guanfacine and Lithium will be very helpful," responded the Doctor.

"More drugs? We have been along that path before and all they do is to make me feel stupid," said Moose.

"Oh, that is what it is. What a relief. We always thought that you were born stupid," said Badger, and all laughed.

Karla came to the room and said to them, "Be nice to Moose, guys. You know he is smart." And to Thurston, "Doctor, I believe your patient is awake."

"Let me go talk to him first, I think we have made a bond of sorts," said Wolf and added, "Rabbit, have that video ready for showtime."

Leopold's healthy arm and both of his legs were tied to the bedpost of the bed he was resting in. His eyes showed a mixture of anger and fear at the sight of the man who had broken his arm.

"Who are you people, and what do you want from me?" he asked.

"Funny those lines are repeated over and over in movies and real life when people find themselves in a situation as difficult as the one you are in now. To the first part of your question, we are the best friends you could possibly find if you want to stay alive."

"I have very powerful friends, you will regret doing this, I will kill you with my own hands."

"Well, Leo, that is very unlikely, number one, because your powerful friends happen to be in deep shit right now. Plus, they know that you actually represent a danger to them, so they are the ones wanting to erase your ugly scared face out of the face of the planet. Second, I do not regret doing this, actually I am enjoying every second of it. Thirdly, I you want to kill me with your own hands, you will have to wait about three months until the broken bones in your arm heal."

"And to the second part of your original question, Leo, we want a full confession of the involvement of General Masters in this plot, your attack on the Mason lady, and the killing of the Chinese couple."

"I believe you are lying. Masters would never do anything to hurt me."

"No? Let me take you to the movies to show you what

153

your dear friend Masters is going to do to you. Rabbit bring the laptop here please."

Rabbit came into the room and, after helping Leopold to sit on the bed, with the help of a couple of pillows, put the laptop on Leo's lap and turned it on. Leopold was obviously impressed and scared.

"Assuming that you guys are not showing me a doctored video and also assuming that I was willing to do what you are asking, what do I get in return?"

"First, you save your life. Second, the people we work for may get you a plea bargain deal and you may spend only a few years in prison. Third, you save yourself a lot of physical pain, and perhaps another couple of broken bones."

"I tell you what, first I will not testify in person neither before a judge nor before Congress because very likely I get killed before or after doing that. I do not want to go to prison either, but I may be willing to do a full confession by video and sign a paper stating that the confession is real. Second, I want a full pardon, or a passport and a plane ticket to get out of the country. Oh, and a real orthopedic surgeon to fix the arm you broke and that joke of a doctor who tried to fix it."

"Not to Russia, I suppose, and of course you want, the best orthopedist in the country, and how about a million dollars on top of that?" said Rabbit, and Wolf smiled.

"No, not to Russia or any country near it, but Mexico, Brazil, Argentina, and even Canada sound attractive. Otherwise, a confession obtained under duress from a man you kidnapped would be thrown away by any judge, and you would not kill me because you need me. That is the problem with you Americans and your judicial system. In Russia, we will do things differently, faster, and cheaper"

"We will submit your proposal to our superiors for consideration, and, of course, even if they accept it probably be some modifications and amendments to your request," said Wolf.

"As long those amendments and modifications are reasonable, I am willing to listen. Meanwhile, can you say to that quack of a doctor to give me some more pain medication?"

"The doctor is gone, and he said to give you only Tylenol or Advil. So that is what you will get."

"Can you at least give me some Vodka to swallow it?"

"We do not have Vodka but may have some whiskey. We will give you some."

"See, you Americans don't even know what is best to drink."

Rabbit gave him a couple of ounces of bourbon in a glass along with the analgesic, checked the restraints, and left.

Wolf called General Silvia Fuentes-Graham, and she, in turn, reported to Senator McClain.

The Senator was not happy with the proposition, but time was running short. The House of Representatives was going to meet in two days, despite the demonstrations and clashes with police, and it was almost certain that they would vote for an impeachment by a wide majority, probably within a day or two.

But thereafter, the Senate would have to vote again, and the President had strong support there. Yet McClain was sure that in spite of that, considering the seriousness of the crime, the majority would vote for impeachment, but the procedures would most likely take longer than a week, maybe two.

So, Wolf was called, given the message, and Leopold was informed that the video confession was acceptable, that he would not have to stand trial or go to prison, and that someone would just drive him to the other side of the border with Mexico and leave him there.

Leopold agreed, much to the chagrin of all members of the team who wanted to put a bullet in the guy's head.

Leopold stated on the video that he had no knowledge of POTUS involvement—which was actually true, and that the killing of the Chinese couple was due to a misunderstanding and actually to lack of information because he had no prior knowledge that the man was being called to the White House. If he knew that the Chinese doctor was required by the president, he would have told him so and the guy would have probably come willingly and without any trouble.

He did not know that there was a little girl in the house—

Percy D. Kepfer

also true—and, of course, he pretended that he was sorry and wanted the real culprit to be caught and punished.

The Zoo team thought it was all bullshit.

Chapter 30
RIOT

The morning of the first day of the impeachment hearings from the House of Representatives was grey and cloudy, with light but persistent rain. Because of the demonstrations, which took place mostly in front of the White House, the event had already been delayed three days, so the Representatives decided to start in spite of that and because the crowds had become smaller. Once the impeachment hearings started, it was expected that the crowds would grow and move to the Capitol.

Security at the Capitol had been reinforced, not only in manpower but also in technology. The Capitol police had been given new electronic badges that were to be changed daily, and the same was done for members of the press. There were additional security cameras and facial recognition scans had been installed. There were snipers on the roof of the Capitol. City police in riot gear stood on the steps of the Capitol, and the National Guard was ready, waiting in several school buses only a few blocks away. It was hoped that if the demonstrators did not turn violent, the city and capitol police could handle the crowds without the assistance of the National Guard.

The Zoo squads, minus the women, were among the crowd, with Rabbit and the Patel cousins posing as reporters scanning and filming the event. They all communicated with each other via small devices on their ears.

Moose found it a bit complicated to blend in, being over six feet tall, very muscular, square-faced, with a shaved head and the dark complexion that people from the Caribbean islands usually have.

Wolf, with his thin countenance and pale complexion, green sharp eyes, and handsome face, toppled with salt and pepper hair chopped military style found it easier to blend in, especially since all were wearing rain ponchos, as most people in the crowd were.

Badger, the shortest and chubbiest of the group, would have been the least conspicuous of the group if it wasn't for curly hair, which he tried to keep as short as possible without going military style.

Rabbit was the first to note and reported to the others: "crowd is getting larger with POTUS supporters. I think it is strange because that is the group that has been shrinking the most over last few days."

"Roger to that," was the answer from Wolf, who seemed to have taken command of the group. "Do you see weapons under some ponchos?"

"Not sure but I think so. Wait a minute. I see a face that we saw at the Lincoln Memorial."

"A Ruskie? What is he doing here? Do you think they thought Leopold would be here and would attempt to extract him? I don't think they are that stupid."

"Wait again. I see the guy who shot those Ruskies in the head at Leopold's garage. They are General Master's guys."

"How did the Russians know that the guys who killed their buddies would be here today? An educated guess?"

"Either that or perhaps they took a prisoner and made him talk."

"I did not see that in the video. You guys think it is a confrontation?" asked Rabbit.

"I hope not, there are a lot of innocent civilians here that could be hurt."

"Whatever happens do not interfere, and above all, no firearms."

"Roger to that, Wolf."

The crowds were getting more excited. Both sides were shouting insults at each other and at the Congressmen as well. One group was accusing them of not having enough cojones to throw the rascals out of the White House and the other accusing them of being traitors to the Constitution and wanting to do a coup-de-Etat.

There were physical altercations, and as some police

officers had to come down the steps to break the fights, there were some arrests. Soon, rocks and empty bottles started to be hurdled at the police, and a patrol car was set on fire.

Then there was a shot, and one of the officers on the steps of the Capitol felt, blood coming out of his right thigh. Some officers returned fire, and several people fell, some intentionally trying to protect themselves. Others because they were wounded or dead.

One of Master's men pulled the pin off a hand grenade and hurled it to the cops. However, he was seen by one of the sharpshooters on the roof, who shot him in the head. He died before hitting the floor, but the grenade hit the lower steps of the Capitol and rolled back into the crowd.

There was an explosion, and blood and body parts mixed with the rain.

The riot police were descending the steps, and there was panic with people running away as fast as they could, some falling and being trampled by those running behind.

Paramedics, from the many ambulances standing by, could not move from their vehicles, less be trampled by the running mob.

The National Guard was coming out of the buses and heading toward the running mob. In the confusion, they thought that the mob was coming to attack them, and some fired their weapons, causing more casualties.

The enhancement group stayed put till Wolf gave the order: "Let's get the fuck out of here before we get killed."

They all complied, except Moose, who said, "Just give me a minute, guys. I will catch you later. There is something I must do."

General Master's men were also scrambling to leave, some dropping the weapons that they had concealed under the rain ponchos, as the Russians did the same.

Moose located the man who appeared to have been the leader of the raid at Leopold's shop and grabbed him by the poncho, making him spin and face him. His fist hit the man's face, and he staggered. Moose hit him again and this time he was totally knocked out. Without apparent effort, Moose picked him up, put him over his shoulder and ran after the Russians, catching up with them as they were about to board their SUVs and drop the unconscious man in front of them.

"Here, fellows, I believe that you all were looking for this guy. Take him as a present from the Zoo team. We do not like guys who execute their prisoners. In exchange, I would appreciate a ride out of here as fast as possible because I believe none of us want to be arrested. I will only be for a few blocks, if you don't mind."

The Russians were surprised; they said nothing but made room for Moose in one of the SUVs while putting the unconscious fellow in the trunk of another.

And they all drove away.

Chapter 31
THE AFTERMATH

Small riots occurred throughout the day and into the evening, but by midnight, the city was quiet, and order had been reestablished.

Vehicles had been gutted, some shops had been looted, and a gas station convenience store had been vandalized and torched, but overall, the material damage had been mild.

The human cost was very different.

About twenty-five people died, six of them killed by the explosion of the grenade, ten more were trampled to death by the running mobs, and the rest were victims of firearms. Among those were three police officers.

More than two hundred people had been hurt, counting only those who were hospitalized. Hundreds more were treated and released. Several of the victims were in critical condition. Hundreds more had been arrested. And nobody knew exactly who was to be blamed.

One side accused the other and the authorities were cautious about putting the blame on one group or another. They were putting together the information collected by the multiple cameras located at different sites.

The Zoo team was convinced that the group connected to the guy who threw the grenade was the initiator, and he was most likely a minion of General Masters. That was only a theory, but Moose told the group that he had done a favor to Leopold's Russians, and they had promised to obtain the information from "an asset that they had extracted."

Moose, exercising his discretion, chose not to disclose that he had been the extractor. He did not think that they needed to know that and felt that General Fuentes-Graham probably would not approve of it.

Chapter 32
IMPEACHMENT

The riots delayed the impeachment hearings at the House of Representatives for three days. When they finally recombined, it only took one day to reach a verdict with a record quorum attendance of all 435 Representatives.

The recordings and videos were played several times and only few witnesses were interviewed: Kelly Carter being the key witness, followed by Vincenso Batagliari, Senator James McClain—who, although not called to testify, volunteered to do so, Doctor Joe Thurston and Doctor Lidia DelToro.

It was the last witness, Lidia, who literally put the last nail on the coffin.

Lidia, instead of defending herself, telling her side of the story or responding directly to the questions asked to her, went on the offensive with an impressive tirade.

She blatantly accused the Representatives of being stupid and saying that they should be ashamed of what they were doing, not recognizing their President, herself, and Doctor Chin-Ghan-Do, as Avatars that only had in mind the salvation of the world. Didn't they realize that the biggest problem facing humanity was overpopulation? Didn't they realize that people were destroying the planet? Didn't they realize that it was the poorest and the most uneducated beings the ones that reproduced the most? Didn't they realize that the very poor were suffering because of their uncontrolled multiplication which was the very cause of their poverty? Didn't they know that the leading cause of crime was poverty? Didn't they know how much it costs to support the elderly, the disabled, the person with terminal, untreatable or incurable illness? Didn't they know how much it cost to combat crime and to keep people in jail?

"Sure, yes, I developed the virus hoping to correct those problems or, at least to make a dent on them. But also we developed a vaccine to protect those worth being protected.

"You ladies and gentlemen should know better that anyone the cost of Welfare, Disability, Social Security, assistance to poor countries etc., etc., etc.," she said and continued:

"I wanted to trim a herd that is in dire need to be trimmed in order to save our planet and the human race.

"Doctor Chin was also a visionary, like me. Between the two of us. we perfected the virus to make it more selective in its attack to the reproductive system. And again, we developed a vaccine to be able to stop it, in case it went out of control.

"Obviously you people do not understand, as did many people we presented our project to, before we met General Charles Masters who, immediately saw the benefits of our ideas and offered not only financial aid but also to set up a meeting with big pharma and the President."

"That was because they saw the potential for large profit, is that correct?" asked the chairman of the committee.

"Perhaps, but I believe that it is only fair that they make a profit on their investment. I do not think it is cheap to make vaccines to administer to most of the population of the world.

"All those people are good people and should be regarded as heroes instead of their character and honesty being challenged in this circus."

"Dr. DelToro, did you ever consider that such project amounted to genocide in a scale not seen since the days of Hitler and the Nazis?"

"I knew that someone was going to come up with that line and the answer is no, the Nazis targeted the elimination of an entire race. My project favors the whole human race equally for all races, religions and flags."

"With your pardon, I fail to see the difference, Doctor. Can you tell us where the virus is now?" asked the chairman.

"I suppose it is still in my laboratory, where I had it before Dr. Thurston kidnapped me."

Doctor Thurston spoke up: "The virus has been destroyed, Mr. Speaker. I considered it too dangerous and too risky to allow it to fall in the wrong hands. So I put it on Dr.

DelToro's laboratory microwave and left it to cook at 200 degrees centigrade for thirty minutes."

"You did what? You are a stupid, stupid joke of a scientist... You destroyed what was perhaps the last hope for the human race to survive and continue thriving!" exploded Dr. DelToro.

"Dr. DelToro, do you expect to save the human race by killing thousands, perhaps millions of people? I am sorry to repeat it, but that sounds very Nazi to me," said the Speaker.

"I am not a Nazi. I am not a Nazi sympathizer. I am a proud American. My virus was not developed to kill people. The idea, that you people do not seem to comprehend, is that it was supposed to sterilize mostly those who reproduce without awareness or concern. If the virus makes some people sick and may cause some deaths, that could be considered collateral damage, which, if you think about it, offsets the number of babies that are killed each year by legal abortion.

"That would be another advantage of my serum. If there are no pregnancies, there would be no abortions. And abortions, ladies and gentlemen, are legal murder in this country.

"The flu kills about 100 people a day in the US alone during flu season. We have a vaccine for it, yet we cannot totally prevent people from catching it and dying from it.

"Our president and few other people were the only one's smart enough to understand the idea, and if in the process of putting it in practice they or someone else was going to make some money, so be it. I believe they deserved to be rewarded."

"It seems to us that, regretfully, you are totally convinced of your ideas, as crazy as they sound to us, anyone's ideas are protected by the First Amendment of the Constitution of the United States. However, the development of what I consider a weapon of mass destruction and the intent to commit genocide are not protected and are considered a crime under the laws of the United States of America and, probably by the laws of any other civilized country in the world. Dr. DelToro, have you ever been diagnosed with any type of mental problem? You lived Africa for a while. Did you contacted malaria, or any other disease that may affect the normal functioning of the brain?"

"Are you asking me if I am crazy? Perhaps you are by not seeing the brilliance of my ideas. But again, through history most great men and women have been considered crazy."

"So, Doctor, you consider yourself a genius?" asked the Speaker.

"I would not go that far, but I would ask you to look at my record, Mr. Speaker."

"Thank you. That will be enough, Dr. DelToro. This assembly will recommend that you submit yourself to a psychiatric evaluation and also be turned to the Homeland Security authorities to be charged with crimes against the people of the United States."

Of the 435 Representatives, oddly, only 35 voted against the impeachment and 10 abstained, 390 voted in favor, a majority hardly ever seen before in the history of the United States of America.

Then the articles of impeachment went to the Senate for confirmation.

The hearings there took several days longer. They called the same witness. Dr. DelToro repeated her tirade almost to the letter. Kelly Carter's veracity was questioned often, and she was close to being called a traitor by some Senators.

Was she involved with the President? Was she jealous?

Did she have grudges against the President, the Vice-President, or the Chief of Staff?

Did she have political ambitions?

Did she know Lieutenant Batagliari before? Did she pay him to confirm her story?

They nailed her to the point of crying, some simply out of meanness because they had always resented her for being so close to the President; others because she had publicly criticized their actions or ideas. But at the end of the day, most believed her story.

They called the CEOs of the big pharmaceutical companies, who came accompanied by a legion of lawyers who swore that all their clients did was to come to a meeting at the White House to hear a proposition related to the development of a vaccine for a new virus. When confronted with the evidence presented and recorded in the flash drive, most just took the Fifth Amendment.

They called Leopold Mishanivich a liar, and the defense lawyers for the White House first questioned and then discarded the confession he made on the tape because it could have been obtained under duress or even torture.

Not Senator McClain, nor Silvia, nor Wolf could talk Leopold into coming to testify in person. He claimed that he had been offered a way out in exchange for the confession he made on tape and that, if forced to go in person, he would deny everything and claim that he had been tortured to say what he said on the tape.

The best he could do was to make an additional video in front of a public place, in the middle of the night, with no public present and one lawyer from each side present while he presented himself clean, well-dressed, and shaved, confirming everything that he said in the first tape.

Afterward, he wanted to be taken to Mexico.

They had no choice but to agree, and yet the prosecution lawyers had difficulty convincing the Senate to admit both videos as evidence.

The Senate did not call the President or Vice-President as witnesses. However, they called the Chief of Staff, General Charles Flynn Masters, who was nailed for two straight days.

In the end, along with Dr. DelToro, he appeared to be the guiltiest in the whole ordeal. Leopold Mishanivich was condemned in absentia, and all three were recommended to be arrested and judged in a court of law.

However, the simple fact that the president had considered participating in the deal and the fact that there were several deaths suspiciously related to the project made the majority of the Senators vote in favor of impeachment.

Yet, the tally was not unanimous. Out of the 100 Senators, 78 voted in favor of impeachment, which was above the 60% required, 12 voted against and 10 abstained.

The President and Vice-President of the United States had been impeached for the first time in the history of the country. With that verdict, they would be removed from their positions, lose their pensions and benefits, would not have the protections of the Secret Service and be subject to civil or criminal prosecution.

The deposed POTUS had been reelected and was serving the first six months of his second term in office.

The Chief Justice of the Supreme Court was called to swear in the Speaker of the House as the next president. The Speaker will hold the post until the next election in three-and-a-quarter years.

Chapter 33
A.S.P.

By now, the cabin in the woods belonging to Karla Messer and her husband had become the headquarters of the Zoo team, and that was where Leopold Mishanivich was being held.

When Moose returned, he told the team that someone gave him a ride to a Wawa gas station, where he told them he had left his car. From there, he called an Uber to drive him to a spot about five miles from the cabin. He did this because he had only a few dollars left of the money that Professor Thurston had given him for expenses and, of course, also he did not want anyone to know the location of the cabin.

Not long after his return, after he had taken a shower and had a ham and cheese sandwich, his cell phone rang.

The conversation was brief and then he addressed those present, including Vince and Professor Thurston.

"It was one of Leopold's Russian friends. They apparently apprehended one of the fellows who killed their friends at the auto shop and made him talk in exchange for a quick and painless death instead of a slow and painful one."

Moose paused, smashed the cell phone, and hurled it into the middle of the nearby lake, then asked the group, "Has anyone heard of a security company called ASP?"

Everyone shook their head in a negative way

"Nobody?" Neither have I, but apparently our friend Leopold is familiar with it, so let's ask him."

"Speaking of Leopold," said Dr. Thurston, "The specimen that I analyzed confirms he got the enhancement serum at some point. However, the changes in his cells are not as marked as they are in you guys, which makes me think that he did not get the full three doses."

"Interesting, if we could find out," said Vince.

"He is not much of a talkative guy," interlocked Wolf,

"unless there is either reward or punishment."

"And he is not the bravest kid in the block," said Moose.

"Two of you will have a chance to find out while driving him to the Mexican border," said Dr. Thurston.

"We will have to drive him? I thought that we were going to fly him over. Why we don't just shoot him in the back of the head and bury him in the woods?" asked Moose.

"No can do. If he flies commercial, he would be identified and arrested. Then he would recant the whole story. Besides those are the orders from General Fuentes," said Dr. Thurston.

"Who will drive him to the border, Doctor?" asked Badger.

"Not you, my friend. Remember you are an escapee from prison? You have to lie low for a while until perhaps we can get a pardon or a reduced sentence for you. As for Wolf and Moose, they are officially under the temporary service of General Fuentes and probably are not allowed to leave the state. So, I guess that leaves Lieutenant Batagliari and Rabbit. But first, let us go talk to Leo about ASP," instructed Dr. Thurston.

"Oh, you found out about ASP, and you thought good old Leopold was going to give you information about it for free? Yes, I am very familiar with ASP; I will give you all the information you want about it when I am on my way to the Mexican border, after my visit to the orthopedist, treatment for my arm, a passport, some money for the trip and at least couple of changes of clothes."

"You ask for a lot, Leo. We can get the information elsewhere, shoot you in the head, and bury you in the woods," said Moose.

"Oh. I know you can do that, but I also know you won't do it. You are not cold-blooded killers. Yes, you may have killed in action, but that is not the same as killing a defenseless human being. Besides, I think Dr. Quack and your pretty bosses would not allow you to do that. Therefore, best to take Leo's offer."

"Okay, you win," said Dr. Thurston. "Let me call an orthopedist friend of mine and see if he can meet us in his office after hours. I believe he takes X-rays in his office. And I'll ask Lioness to go shopping for your clothes."

Dr. Thurston made three phone calls. In addition to the one to his colleague and Karla, he called the senator to make sure that Vince was finished testifying and was free to travel to Mexico with Leopold and Rabbit.

The Orthopedist friend of Dr. Thurston opened his office after hours to accommodate his recommended patient. Two of the boys from the zoo team took him there.

After an x-ray showed that he had sustained a greenstick fracture of the middle shaft of the ulna and the radius. He concluded that Dr. Thurston had done a decent job straightening and holding together the bones. All he did was change the cast and discharge him.

Thereafter, they went back to the cabin to pack for the trip. Rabbit's suitcase contained the clothes that Karla had bought for the three men who were going to make the trip to Mexico. Rabbit also took a cassette and a video recorder.

Moose still thought that it was a bad idea to release the prisoner and preferred the idea of putting a bullet in the back of his head. But, as a soldier, he was used to obeying orders.

They were to drive a rental car on Route 81, then 40 to Little Rock, finally 30 to El Paso, and lastly, Ciudad Juarez, on the other side of the border. Leopold had made it very clear that he would not start talking until they were at least in Kentucky, so they drove.

Leopold turned out to be very talkative. He did not yet give information about ASP but started telling them about himself. He was born in St. Petersburg, Russia, the third of six children, five of them women. His dad was a high-ranking KGB officer who saw potential in his son to join the ranks.

Unfortunately, Leopold was not very strong as a kid. However, he was very intelligent, had an excellent memory, and, above all, had an extraordinary ability to learn languages. So, by the time he was in college, he was fluent in English, Spanish, and Dari Persian (Farsi), and he could make himself understood in French and Italian—all these, in addition to his native Russian.

So it was because of these abilities that the KGB embraced him and also why they sent him to Afghanistan, where he realized that there was an enormous potential to make tons of money in the contraband of poppy flowers to make opium and heroin. And tons of money he made up until the KGB found out about his business and raided his compound, confiscating all the money he had stashed there and killing or capturing most of his operatives.

By sheer luck, he was not there that night, but he knew that he could no longer stay in Afghanistan, nor could he return to the motherland. Therefore, he decided that the best and safest way was to defect to the Americans. The KGB knew about a covert operation by an American military unit operating on the border with Pakistan, who supplied arms and logistics to the Taliban and whose commander was a man named Charles Flynn Masters, and he turned himself in to him.

"I did not have a shit ton of information to give to the man, but it was not difficult to convince him that I was a very valuable Russian asset who had tons of secret information to give to America once I was on American soil. Masters was so eager to make a name for himself and, also, to get out of that shithole that he swallowed the hook, the lure, and the sinker.

"But you know what the funniest thing was?" He did not expect an answer. "The CIA bought my shit as well. It took them several months to realize that they already knew most of the staff I gave them, and some more were just fibs that I made up."

They had been driving most of the day, and they were tired, hungry, and sleepy. They were already in Kentucky, so they checked into a motel and called for pizza and soda to be delivered to their room.

"I promise that tomorrow you hear the next chapter of the story, the one with the ASP on it. But tonight I want you to give me a couple of those pain pills that the ortho path prescribed and then want to go to sleep."

He swallowed the two pills with a gulp of soda, lay down in the bed, and was snoring less than five minutes later.

"I don't know how this guy can sleep after all the crimes he has committed. I still have trouble with that, and it was war then," said Rabbit.

"If it is any consolation, I do too. You go try to sleep, Leroy," said Vincent to Rabbit. "I do not trust this guy, even with broken arm and legs tied to mine. He is a snake. I'll take the first watch and wake you in about four hours."

Rabbit gave no arguments, and he also fell asleep as soon as he hit the pillow.

Vincenso was thinking of how much his life had changed since the day he met the woman in the green dress. Thanks to her, he found the answers he had been looking for and also had found something that he thought had lost forever: a purpose in life and, perhaps, a new family.

Exactly four and a half hours later, Leroy woke up and completed the rest of the night watch, understanding that Vincent would be the first driver of the day. Vince woke up at seven, shaking slightly to wake Leopold, who was still under the effect of the analgesic he had taken the previous night.

After taking a shower and a light breakfast at the motel lobby, they went back on the road.

"We are ready to hear the rest of the story, Leo. If you don't tell us, there will be no more painkillers for you."

"Okay, fellows. I am a man of my word. Let me see where I was last night?"

"You fooled General Masters and the CIA to get admitted to this county."

"Right, and they treated me very nicely. First they put me in fancy hotels, then in military facilities. And when eventually they realized that I did not have any useful information, they just let me loose.

"I had no money, so I worked some menial, minimal-wage jobs and slept in homeless shelters until I decided to approach Flynn Masters again, and he got me a job at ASP.

"Of course, I had to twist his arm a little by telling him that I would tell the CIA he knew all along that I was not a valuable asset to bring to the USA, and I went further by threatening to tell the FBI that he had been in the poppy flower business with me. It was a bluff and a long shot and he could have had me killed, but somehow it worked.

"It got an entry-level job at ASP, and I did not know at the time that Masters was a major stockholder of ASP or that ASP was a big corporation holding government security contracts and other types of contracts (if you know what I mean?), for cartels or rich people that could afford their fees. Otherwise, it was a legit business offering security to stores, banks, warehouses, and protection to rock and movie stars, hot shit executives, etc.

"What I learned later and found most interesting was that the Board of Directors of ASP was made exclusively of members of Masters' old squad, which originally numbered fourteen. So fifteen is the number of chairs in the boardroom.

Actually, now is only thirteen because two died in action. Not sure where those casualties occurred because there were fourteen when I left Afghanistan with Masters' men staying behind. Perhaps it happened then."

"I thought that we were not involved in the fight in Afghanistan at that time," said Vince.

"We were, and we weren't. We were supposed to offer intelligence, logistics, and arms to the Taliban without getting involved. But Masters and his men found that boring. So, often, they stripped off their uniforms, pretended to be Russians, or Taliban, and raided small villages. They did it especially if there was a wedding taking place there, as the bride and her maids usually wore expensive jewelry. They went into the towns, killed the men, raped the women, and at times killed them as well, and walked away with anything valuable. They found it valuable that I spoke Russian and Farsi, so they took me with them in a few of their raids".

"So, you are going to make us believe that you were just an innocent bystander? That is a bunch of fucken shit," said Vincent.

"I didn't say I was an innocent bystander. But I swear that I did not kill or rape anyone. I may have taken money and jewelry, but that was about it. And I do not give crap about whether you believe me or not. That is in the past.

"The Russians are gone from Afghanistan. Now you are entangled in a war there that has lasted twenty years and counting because your friends, the Taliban, became your enemies and used the stingers you gave them against your own helicopters. And, oh yes, they helped the guy who blew up the Twin Towers in New York City. So much for the enemy of my enemy is my friend. I bet you been there in that shithole and saw it for yourself."

"That is politics. I am a soldier and was trained not to question my orders," said Vince.

"That is exactly what the Nazis said at Nuremberg.... They hung them anyway. And you should not be so cocky about the soldier thing because ASP probably has you in the crosshairs."

"Me? Why?" asked Vince.

"Not only you, the Carter woman, the Quack Doctor, and maybe even the Senator. Why, because you all helped to destroy the career of one of their own."

Leopold paused here to comment on Leroy-Rabbit-Smith snoring. "Maybe even your noisy friend here would be in danger, as I am now certain that I am. You see, Lieutenant, the ASP squad of fifteen pledged that whoever did any harm to any of their members in any scenario other than combat would be avenged by the others wherever and whoever they may be. That is why they keep the chairs of those gone empty but still around the table."

"Can they quit if they want, or retire?"

"It is my understanding that they can and receive a hefty severance pay—plus continue being shareholders—provided that they never, ever discuss with anyone, other than the members, anything related to the organization."

"How come you were able to quit?" asked Vince.

"I was never part of the organization, not even a sicario. Those sign a non-disclosure agreement and can quit like in any other job, as long as they are not too deep in. Those who are deeply involved with illegal actions do not want to talk because they incriminate themselves. I was just a minor peon and was also doing some business on the side. So then one day I was caught and sent to prison.

"While there, someone offered me ten thousand dollars if I was willing to participate in an experiment. Something related to a serum that would make me something like Capitan America.

"I found out later that Masters had hired two doctors who had developed a medicine, a serum that was supposed to make people strong. These guys used to work for the government. I believe their names were Colton and Pratt, but they had been fired. I did not know for what reason at the time. So me and another fellow—a big, burly guy, but not very smart—accepted the offer and submitted to the experiment.

"The other guy went first, actually two weeks ahead of me; we were supposed to get three doses of the dammed thing. He had gotten two and seemed okay. So I went for my first dose the same day that he went for his third."

Leopold took a sip from a bottle of water and continued. It seemed like he could not stop talking now that he had started. Rabbit was awake now and checked that the recording equipment had been working okay all along.

Leopold continued: "We were in different rooms, separated by a wall of Plexiglas, so I could see the other room where the big guy was getting his IV infusion. That was the main lab and the two doctors were there. All of a sudden, something that one of the doctors said or did, pissed off the big guy. He grabbed the doctor by the throat, smashed his face with his big fist, and threw him clean across the room. I am pretty sure he was dead.

"The other doctor could not get out because the door was on the other side of the room, and the big guy was charging at him. So the doctor grabbed something, some flammable liquid, and threw it at the big guy. But he was already on the doctor, so he turns his lighter and sets the big guy on fire. The guy still smashes the head of the doctor against a table, then he is ablaze and starts running all over the lab, screaming bloody murder and setting the whole place on fire."

Another pause from Leopold, who now was sweating as if he was having a nightmare.

"The big guy is now a fireball, and he is approaching the Plexiglas divide that is now beginning to melt. So I get up, pull the IV out of my arm and look for an escape. There is no way I can reach the door because it is at the other end of the lab. There is a window, but it is closed. So I grab a chair, smash the glass and jump thru it. The back of my clothes were on fire already, so I jump through the window and cut my face with the glass. Then I realized that the fucken lab is in a second story building. Luckily I landed on a garbage dumpster, which, unluckily had the lid closed. So I smashed my head and passed out. Woke up in a hospital three days later with second and third-degree burns on my butt and back, which kept me in the hospital for over a month."

"Then what happened to you after that?" asked Vince and Rabbit almost at once.

"Well, not a damn soul from ASP came to visit. However, they paid my hospital bills, and I got the ten thousand dollars that they had offered me, which helped me start my own business."

"Did you notice any changes in your physics or behavior? You said that serum was supposed to make you Captain America," Said Rabbit.

"For sure, it did not make me Captain America. However, I don't know if it was the serum or the concussion, but yes, I noticed some changes. For one, I was able to perfect my French and my Italian and started learning Mandarin."

"Is that it?" Vince and Rabbit insisted.

"I became hornier, which is not good when you are not married and you have an ugly scar across your face. Are you guys married? Bet you have hot wives, right?" he said, laughing.

Rabbit slapped him across the face and told him to remain silent the rest of the day unless he had some more pertinent information to give.

They reached El Paso before midnight and decided to spend the night there before crossing to Ciudad Juarez the following morning to discharge Leopold at a hotel there.

Chapter 34
EXECUTIVE PARDONS

The day before the Senate confirmed the President's impeachment, the White House was busier than usual, with lawyers, senators, presidential staff, and politicians traveling between the House and the Capitol.

The President had had very little sleep in the nights preceding the final verdict, and so did the Vice-President and, much less so, General Masters.

By a prior agreement, the lawyers of POTUS and Vice-POTUS had concluded that the best thing for them was to blame General Masters for all the crimes and murders, making him their scapegoat, a deal he had agreed with in exchange for two-thirds of the amounts of money they were collecting for the President Defense Fund, which now amounted to well over three hundred million dollars. That money was to be deposited in a Swiss bank account. Also, he asked for a full executive pardon for the federal offenses and the possibility of a plea bargain for the state crimes.

The President also extended full pardons to the CEOs of the big Pharma Companies. However, their lawyers, although keeping the document for a "just in case use" preferred not to use them because accepting a pardon would be considered admission of guilt.

POTUS pardoned himself and the Vice President, a move unprecedented in the history of the United States, and the validity of which would be debated for months and years before the president could be formally charged with any crime.

Additionally secret plans were being made for the exit of General Masters who "no way, no how" was going to go to prison, even for one day. Therefore, after hearing the recommendation of the Senate regarding his arrest, he left the Senate floor in a hurry, flanked by his lawyers and security, disappeared into the tunnels under the Capitol, and emerged to be picked up by an SUV that was waiting for him.

The SUV took him to the headquarters of ASP, where he transferred his assets to a Swiss bank account and thereafter a helicopter flew him to a safe house belonging to the ASP company.

Masters summoned the members of his squad to meet with him at a safe house. The men were now in their mid-50s, some balding, some with gray hair, but most still in good shape and health, as they continued doing regular exercise and trying to stay fit.

There were only eleven

"Where is Stephen?" asked Masters

"Don't know," was the response. "We have not seen him since the day of the riot. But that is not unusual, we don't see each other every day."

"Yup, we only see everyone during the monthly meeting and at parties or special occasions," answered a guy named Mike.

"Has anyone called his house? I did when I called this meeting, and there was no answer," said Masters

"He has lived alone since his divorce. A housekeeper comes over a few times per week but, as far as I know, they not always cross paths."

"I think someone should go check at his home. He may have been hurt during the riot," said Masters.

"We have seen the list of the people dead, hurt or arrested, and his name is not in any of those. I know that he definitely was not the guy who threw the grenade. He was one of our guys, a rookie and that was clumsy," said another.

"Well, I hate to start a meeting without the whole squad being present, but this is a special occasion and a special meeting.

"As you well know the shit has hit the fan at the White House and I was the one who took the punch for the boss. I was expecting to be impeached. I was expecting to be accused of conspiracy, probably facing removal of my military grade. But it turns out that I am accused of conspiracy to commit genocide, and the murders of several people; so I am supposed to be going the prison, and all because of that treasonous bitch Kelly Carter."

"We take it that you want her dead, Commander. If that is so, consider it done," said a third.

"Of course, I want her death but not only her. I want to kill that Italian guy who helped her, that Dr. Thurston and Senator McClain. I would love to see their corpses before I leave this country for the tropics"

"Do you have a plan, Commander?" asked Mike.

"Yes, I do, but first I want to sell my shares of ASP. You know they are trading at forty-four dollars a share as of yesterday. I have twenty thousand shares. I will sell them to you for twenty-five, and you can re-sell for at least forty. I would love it if each one of you buys some, ideally equal parts."

"With all due respect, Commander, after this scandal, with your name in the company roster, the value of the shares will likely plummet," said another man.

"True, but so far, nobody, other than you guys, knows that I have an interest in this company. It is very probable that the FBI will start digging and may eventually find out, but by then you would have sold the shares and made big bucks"

"Okay, Commander, we are in. How about Stephen? He probably would get in if he was here?"

"I will save the shares for Stephen when he reappears. Make sure you keep looking for him."

"Come on, Commander. You know we will. Our motto is that no man is left behind. I kick myself in the butt for not realizing earlier that he was missing. None of us did."

"Okay, just find the guy. Here is the plan, listen carefully."

Chapter 35
CIUDAD JUAREZ

Leopold Mishanivich checked in to one of the best hotels in Ciudad Juarez. He was in Mexico, on the other side of the border. He felt safe now. Even his broken arm, still in a cast, did not hurt anymore.

Leo took a shower, went out for dinner at a nearby restaurant, and made a call with a cheap cell phone that he bought at a local store next to the restaurant. Then, he went back to his room and waited.

Less than two hours later, there was a knock on his door, and two men walked in: "*Usted es el Ruso amigo del Jefe* (Are you the Russian friend of the boss?)?"

"*Si yo soy, quienes son ustedes y donde está El Chapito* (Yes, I am. Who are you and where is Chapito?)?"

Switching to heavy accented broken English, one of the Mexicans said:

"The boss sends his regrets that he was unable to come and greet you in person because he says that right now you are 'a hot potato,' with the FBI, Interpol and the Mexican authorities looking for you. So it would not be wise for him to be seen in your company right now."

"So, I will not be able to see Chapito?" said the Russian with a clear desperation in his voice.

"Yes, not this time, amigo. However, he said that he was willing to help you, so he sent you this." He handed Leo a fat envelope full of money—ten thousand American dollars, to be exact.

"We are supposed to take you to a doctor who will change your appearance and provide you with a passport, and there, in the envelope, is also a plane ticket to Mexico City. The boss hopes That all of these will help you start in the city, where you can easily melt away among the twelve million people who live there."

"Come on. Get ready. *¡Vamonos!*" the man said, while the other was already putting Leo's few belongings into his suitcase.

An old beaten-up pickup truck with faded red paint was waiting outside the hotel. One of the men got into the driver's seat and signaled Leo to take the passenger seat. The other guy stayed behind paying the hotel bill and then got in the back of the truck.

Leopold could not help but notice the two AK47s lying on the floor of the truck. He had already noticed that each one of the men was carrying a weapon tucked under their shirts. Yet, Leopold was not afraid. He actually had a good feeling about the whole thing. He was not even afraid after being told they had to blindfold him.

About fifteen minutes later, they arrived at their destination. He was helped to descend from the truck and guided into a short corridor, his eyes were not uncovered until he was in a well-lighted room and a distinguished-looking gentleman dressed in green surgical scrubs started examining his face, and said in perfect English:

"I am Doctor Carlos, of course not my real name. I am a plastic and reconstructive surgeon. Your friends told me that you are not happy with your appearance and wish to make some changes. Is that correct?"

Leo noticed that the two Mexicans who had brought him there were gone, so he could have said no, but instead, he said yes.

It would be funny, he thought. He got the scar on his face at a place similar to this, with similar-looking doctors and similar ten thousand dollars. Now, he was about to get rid of it…or wasn't he?

As the doctor got closer to his face, he smelled the alcohol on his breath, and yet, in spite of that, he still did not feel like running away from there.

The doctor was explaining the procedure. "First of all, I will be honest with you. Do not keep your expectations too high. That is a big scar with keloid transformation, and even the best cosmetic surgeon in the world would not be able to make it completely disappear.

"What I am going to do is a procedure called dermabrasion, which is basically to sand off the scar, to make it flatter and even with the rest of your face. Then, I am going to inject a steroid into it, to try to keep it from becoming keloid again. Under normal circumstances patients get to wear a compression mask for few days after the surgery in order to keep the scar flat. But you have to leave soon, so that would not be possible.

"Then, a makeup artist will apply makeup over it, a barber will cut and dye your hair, and you will be a totally different person. Have you ever worn contact lenses?"

"Yes, I do not require wearing lenses yet, but at the school I attended they made us wear contacts to change our eye colors. They are uncomfortable, though."

"Perfect, then. We will give you some color for your complexion. Oh, and do not worry. You will receive a light anesthetic, spend the rest of the day and tonight at the clinic, and then someone will drive you to the airport."

After dressing in a hospital gown, Leopold was placed on an operating table with an IV going through his veins. He did not know what happened until a couple of hours later.

He found his face covered with bandages and himself being wheeled into a room. His face burned like his back did when he was burned in the lab fire years before, so he was given another dose of analgesic IV and fell asleep again. He woke up several times during the night and asked for pain medication. However, after the second time, he only got oral Tylenol for pain, which, much to his surprise, found that it helped.

He actually had to spend an extra day at the clinic because the face dressings were still bloody. But on the third day, the doctor gave the order so, the barber and the makeup artist came to work on him.

His face still burned like a son of a bitch when the doctor took the bandages off and stung very severely when they applied the makeup, which was somewhat tattooed in and, therefore, semi-permanent.

Upon discharge, he was given his $10,000, a new passport, and told not to worry. All expenses had been paid by his friends, and a taxi was called to take him to the airport.

On the flight to Mexico City, he thought of melding with the population, disappearing, and starting an honest business. But he also thought about the General who sent his henchmen to kill him after he sent him on a mission that ended badly just because he had not told him the truth. He also thought about the man who broke his arm, which now was no longer in cast but only in a simple, removable splint.

He also thought about the squad of his fellow Russians who probably were being hunted by the ASP people right now.

Chapter 36
ABRUPTED

Soon after Rabbit and Vince dropped Leopold at the hotel in Juarez and headed back to El Paso, they called Dr. Thurston.

General Silvia Fuentes-Graham was actually the commander of the squad, but they were forbidden to call her directly. Her role in the events of the last weeks had been totally extra official, and she could be in trouble if her superiors found out.

Immediately as the doctor answered the phone, Vince realized something was wrong, so he asked precisely, "What is wrong, Doctor?"

The trembling voice at the other end of the line "I need you guys back here as soon as possible if not earlier."

"We are on our way to El Paso airport. We shall drop the rental and take the first available flight to DC. But Doc, be careful and make sure Mrs. Carter is fine. According to the information that Leo gave us, all three of us and maybe even the Senator are in danger."

"It has already happened. Kelly Carter has been kidnapped."

"Oh my God! It was them, the ASP people. They are peons of General Masters. Rabbit recorded the whole story I would try to play it for you over the cell phone. When did it happen? How?"

"Last night, we do not know how she was under police and FBI protection. Masters has vanished. Two police officers and Kelly's husband are dead. An FBI officer is in critical condition at the hospital."

Indeed, Kelly Carter was supposedly very well protected since General Master disappeared. A police patrol car was stationed in front of her home 24/7, with two officers on board. In addition, a patrol car drove around the block every

184

half hour. A female FBI agent was staying in the house, and Kelly's husband was armed.

So how did it happen?

As the two police officers sat in the car, and the patrol cruiser had just passed in front of the house and turned the corner, another car parked about three cars behind. Two uniformed officers got off and walked towards the patrol car. One of them stepped on each side of the patrol car and knocked on the windows. As soon as the windows were down, the fake officers shot the ones in the car with guns equipped with silencers.

Both officers died instantly. The fake officers walked up to the door of the house and rang the bell.

Kelly and the FBI lady were sitting on a couch in front of the television. Kelly's husband was sitting on a Lazy Boy chair nearby. He got up to answer the door and took a Smith Wesson 9mm, which was on a table nearby, with him. He peeped through the visor on the door and saw the two police officers, so he opened the door.

Kelly was not sure what made her husband suspicious of the two officers—perhaps he saw the guns in their hands—but he screamed, "Kelly run" and tried to fire his gun but barely fired at the ceiling as he fell with two bullets into his chest

The FBI woman, yelled, "get behind the couch" as she pulled her gun and fired at the fake police officers, who avoided being hit by hiding in a corner of the room while firing at the woman. The FBI agent had very little protection from the small couch. So she also took two bullets in her chest.

Kelly managed to grab the woman's radio and said, "Help, help husband and officer killed." One of the guys pulled her by the hair, lifting her off the floor, while the other one got behind her and covered her nose and mouth with a rag with chloroform…. And she went out.

The two men carried her to their car, dropped her in the back seat, and drove off.

Chapter 37
RANSOM

As soon as Rabbit and Vincenso returned from Juarez, the whole squad had an emergency meeting at Karla's cabin. It was presided over by General Silvia-Fuentes Graham, who arrived dressed in civilian clothes, jeans, a T-shirt and military boots.

She addressed the group in a very military manner: "As most of you may be aware, last night at about 2200 hours, a group of armed men posing as police officers broke into the home of Kelly Carter. She was abducted, two officers and her husband were killed, and an FBI agent is in critical condition. She is alive because she was wearing a bulletproof vest.

Dr. Thurston has since heard from the kidnappers, and they demanded relatively little money—only one hundred thousand dollars. But here is the catch: They want the money delivered by Dr. Thurston, Lieutenant Batagliari, and Senator McClain, in person, to a place they would indicate one hour before the delivery."

"Is General Masters behind this? I thought he was taken into custody by the FBI," said Vince.

"The Cat man is way behind in the news. Master gave the slip to the FBI and has disappeared," said Wolf.

"Yes, men, Masters is very likely to be behind this, and according to the information that Leopold gave you, probably his men from ASP. Therefore they do not care about the money. They want revenge, and they want the four people most responsible for the downfall of POTUS and his clique: Kelly, Joe, Vince and the Senator," stated Silvia as she continued. "This is a totally voluntary mission and probably a very dangerous—if not suicidal—one. Joe has already agreed to go, but the Senator declined. We know very well that he is not a coward. Besides thinking that our plan is crazy, he firmly believes that the government should not negotiate with criminals. Yet he gave us the ransom money to use as a bait. Also, he has provided a copy of the tape regarding ASP to the FBI. They must be storming their main place now. But I bet neither Kelly nor Masters be there. Okay, that leaves you. Lieutenant Vince. Are you in or not? If you decline, nobody is going to criticize you."

"I am all in, General. However, would they be willing to negotiate if only the two of us show up?"

"Dr. Thurston is supposed to talk to them when they call again, which should be before sixteen hours this afternoon or about four hours from now, and I believe they prefer to have three of the targets rather than just one, the woman.

"Meanwhile, the boys and I have been working on a plan with the help of the Patel cousins. You'll be wearing tiny trackers inside your belts. And I do not mean tucked in your belts, but in between the two layers of leather, so we will track you down from wherever you meet them to wherever they take you. Then the squad will deal with them and get you out, hopefully alive."

"That is not very reassuring, General, but I am confident in you and the Zoo squad."

"We will need a sniper. Badger used to be the best, but with all that shit and booze that he has put into his body through the years, he probably has shaky hands now," said Moose.

"Fuck you, Moose. I have been in jail for three months and been with you guys for almost another month. During all that time I have been sober and clean. I bet I can hit a beer can from a hundred yards—no, make it two hundred yards. But that is irrelevant. We do not have a sniper rifle."

"Yes, we do. I borrowed one from the base with sufficient ammo. It is in the trunk of my car. Make sure you do not lose or damage it. Remember, it is government property. You have an hour to practice, Private Boone, go now," ordered General Silvia.

"So, here is the plan: we use the tracker to follow you to whatever location they have chosen to take you, which most likely is not where they have Kelly. And it is very unlikely that they will kill you there. So they will take you to another place to have the three of you together and have fun with you before killing you, probably one by one."

"That sounds very pleasant, reassuring, and encouraging," said Dr. Thurston.

"We will be there. The trackers are also transmitters. So if we hear that they are going to kill you at the meeting place, we will take them down before that happens. Most likely, they will put hoods on your heads and drive you away to the place where they have Kelly. Then we take them down, rescue all of you, and we all live happily ever after."

Indeed, what could go wrong?

At exactly 1600 hours (4 pm in non-military time), Dr. Joe Thurston's phone rang, and he answered telling them in very tacit terms that the Senator was not coming, only himself and Vincent. If that was not good enough, nobody was coming, and the deal was off.

The man on the other end of the line only argued a bit before saying that he was going to check with the others and call back using a different cell phone in case he intended to track the one he was using.

Five minutes later, he called again and agreed with the doctor and the lieutenant delivering the money and gave the location of a busy strip mall in nearby Virginia. The two were supposed to come alone and wait in front of a supermarket in that plaza. They were not to be accompanied by police, the FBI, or to carry weapons.

The Doctor and Vincent drove to the designated mall, parked the car, walked to the supermarket, and stood by the curb waiting.

Several minutes passed, and several cars, all suspicious to them, passed in front of the place, none stopping.

Then, a middle-aged man wearing a supermarket uniform approached from behind and told them to walk along parking row number seven, ahead of him, as he was pushing a supermarket cart with some groceries. About halfway, there was a black Cadillac SUV with Florida plates, and he told them to open the door and sit in the back. There were two men inside the car, pointing automatic pistols at them. "Lie on the floor, face down," one said.

The supermarket guy approached another car, a Chevy Impala with one man inside, loaded the groceries in the back of the vehicle, removed the uniform shirt, and rode shotgun. The Chevy followed the SUV.

The team was following at a distance, enough to pick up the signal and hear the conversations, but not enough to be detected. The Rabbit was riding in one of the cars and the Patel cousins, one in each of the others, each carrying a sensitive monitor device.

"Since they already have the targets, they will probably drive straight to their hidden place," said Moose, who was driving the car in which General Silvia was riding shotgun.

"I certainly hope so, but I do not believe that it would be that easy. I guess that they will take them to a deserted place, search them, discard the briefcase, minus the money, and then go to their hideout," said General Fuentes-Graham.

After about thirty minutes, the vehicles indeed stopped in front of a dilapidated, abandoned building and got the hostages out, heads covered with black hoods, and took them inside and told them to lie on the floor face down.

The team waited, listening to conversations

The kidnappers weren't very talkative, but Dr. Thurston was, while Vince was trying to control the feeling of "that thing" overwhelming him.

"So, you guys have your money. Why do you need us now? Are you going to kill us here and now?"

"Shut your mouth, or I will break all your teeth with my gun," one of the men said as he slapped the doctor across the face.

That triggered Vince's rage, and in spite of being tied, he got up, head-butted the guy that was closest to him in the face, breaking his nose and kicked the next guy in the groin, making him fall down in pain.

But there were four of them. The two others were out of his reach, and his hands were tied.

One of them hit him in the head with the butt of a

shotgun. As he fell, the other injected something with a needle in his neck.

"This son of a bitch broke my nose. I am going to kill him right here and now."

"You shall not do such thing, soldier. Our orders are to bring them back alive, then the General may allow you to have some fun with them before killing them.

"Come on, you guys. Help me strip these guys in case they are wired. We put their clothes in the briefcase and the money in paper bags. There are several from the supermarket in the Chevy."

The squad had already silently walked towards the place and hidden behind the trees, were observing the site with binoculars. "Did you hear that, General. They are going to strip them. We will lose the tracers. What shall we do now?" asked Rabbit.

For once, General Silvia Fuentes Graham did not have an answer for her men.

Then Badger, who was already out of the car and loading the sniper rifle, saw something flying low near the vehicles of the kidnappers. "What the hell is that boss?" he asked. He was referring to two round objects, the size of a small saucer, that hovered over the bad guy's cars.

"It seems to be a small drone. Actually, there are two of them."

"Shall I shoot them down, boss?"

"No, let's wait. They may answer our problems. Perhaps the FBI launched them. Wait and see what they do."

Once the objects hovered twice over the cars, the drones descended to almost ground level and disappeared under the vehicles, one under each one.

Minutes later, the four men exited the place, pushing roughly one naked man and dragging another who was evidently unconscious, but alive. The team knew it was Vincent because, being totally unconscious, he was not wearing a hood.

"Stupid fool, you could have yourself killed before rescuing anybody," said Silvia.

The naked men were loaded separately in the vehicles and driven off.

The squad noticed that the one guy holding a handkerchief to his bleeding nose was ordered not to ride in the same car as Vince.

The squad had no way to follow the cars without being detected, and they had lost the trackers that were still transmitting from inside the building where Vince's and Doc Thurston's clothes were left, so Moose went inside to get them.

Much to the big guy's surprise, the clothes were gone.

"They took the Doc and Cat clothes with them, commander; the clothes are gone."

"No way, Moose, I was watching them all the time, and I saw nobody carrying any bundle of clothes. Maybe there are some squatters in that old building, and they took them."

Rabbit approached the two from behind and said: "Commander, I am picking up the signal again, but it is coming from the opposite direction that the hostiles took. Wait a minute, the signal is getting stronger, and it is approaching us. It is almost on top of us now."

Not long after Rabbit finished the sentence, four ATVs emerged from the woods at high speed, followed by a black Hummer. A voice came from the trackers and said simply, "Follow."

So, the team ran back to their vehicles, parked hidden in the foliage about a block and a half away, and proceeded to follow the signal from the trackers.

It was late summer or early fall in the areas surrounding the Capital of the US. Therefore the trees had started to change colors and some leaves had started to fall. The sun was beginning to set earlier than a month before, and it was beginning to get dark. It would be night in less than one hour, and they did not dare turn the lights of their vehicles on until they reached a paved road.

The signal was still strong. Whoever had the trackers was not too far away. Hopefully, these people, whoever they were, were playing on the same team as theirs, and hopefully, they will be still on time to save the lives of their comrades

They drove past several unpaved entrances into the woods. At one point, the signal was getting weaker, so the Patels realized that whoever they were following had entered one of those trails that they had left behind. They had to turn back and try again, couple of times until they found the right trail. It was not a long trail, but very narrow and it was hard to stay on the path with the lights of the vehicles off. They realized that had only one pair of night vision goggles.

One pair was worn by Silvia, who rode in the first car and directed her driver. The other cars just had to follow carefully.

Perhaps three-quarters of a mile later, light came from a compound with several log cabins, which appeared to be deserted. At the center was a two-story cabin, and the SUVs, plus two other cars, were parked in front.

Silvia ordered the cars to stop and the squad members to get out, with the exception of the Patel cousins, who were ordered to stay in the car, armed with automatic pistols just in case. There was a gate, which appeared to be unlocked. Silvia told the team to be careful and look for booby traps, antipersonnel mines, etc.

Badger took his sniper rifle, looked for a high, hidden, and covered position, and said to Silvia: "There are no hostiles in the cars, as far as I can see. There is one in the balcony in front of the house and two guarding the main door. They all carry M-16s but do not seem to be worried about anything."

"Can you take them, Badger?"

"I can take the one on the balcony and one of the guys at the front door, but there is no way I can take all three without making them aware of our presence here. Some of our men need to take the other guy in the front. I'll take the one on the left. Maybe Wolf can take the other."

"Roger to that, but Wolf needs to get close to that fellow and I am sure that at least two others are guarding the rear of the house. We have to be completely silent."

"At your command, Commander."

"Let's go then."

Chapter 38
TORTURE AND UNCERTAINTY

Inside the two-story house at the center of the compound, were seven men. Five were part of the ASP directive and two were soldiers. Two of those were the ones who drove the hostages to the place. One was the one with the broken nose, that was still bleeding and getting more swollen by the minute.

"Go put some ice in that face of yours, Joe. You're getting uglier by the minute," joked General Charles Flynn Masters.

Kelly Carter was tied to a chair in the center of the room, her clothes thorn and dirty. Evidently she had been hit in the face several times, as her face was quite swollen, her left eye almost shut and purple. She was in a daze, and did not seem to be totally aware of what was going on around her.

"So this guy did that to him?" Masters said while kicking the abdomen of the still unconscious Vince.

"You stupid fool. He can't feel what you do to him. Don't you see he is under effect of some shit your men injected into him!" shouted Dr. Thurston

"Perhaps he will not feel it, but I am sure you do, my dear doctor," he said, while brutally kicking him in the abdomen and then in the head. The room seemed to spin around and he felt like vomiting.

"Oh, boss, there is some good news and some bad news. Which one you want to hear first?" asked one of the ASP guys.

"Always the good ones first, my boy, always the best first."

"Okay, we have purchased all your shares at twenty-five dollars each and the money has been transferred, along with the money donated by the President, to your bank account in the Caiman Islands."

"That is great news. What is the bad?"

"Stephen has been located. His body was found floating in the Potomac with a bullet to the back of his head."

"Shit, poor Stephen. He did not live to enjoy this party today. Back of the head bullet. Sounds like KGB execution. Perhaps our friend Leopold is behind it. I suppose you would not know where our friend Leo is, Doctor. After all, he made those videos for you?" And he kicked him again.

"You see, Doc? We are only waiting that your Italian friend wakes up for the real party to start. First, we are going to screw that treacherous bitch until everyone in this camp had his turn. Then we are going to cut her tits off and, if she still is alive, I may feel compassionate and put a bullet in her little head. And the two of you are going to watch every minute of it. And once she is done, we will start cutting the Italian up, with you being the last and perhaps the luckiest because by then we may be too tired."

The men in the room laughed and the one with the broken nose requested to be the first to cut Vincent. He wanted to start with his nose, then his dick

"Be patient, my boy. I believe you earned it, so it is granted."

Outside it was dark already, Badger's hands did not shake when he fired the first shot hitting the guy in the balcony in the middle of the forehead. He fell without a sound. Then he aimed for the guy at the right side of the door, which was Badger's left, with same result.

As the man fell, the one on the left of the door reacted. By then Wolf, who had already been in position behind one of the SUVs, threw his knife with the usual accuracy, hitting the guy right in the Adams apple. The man chocked on his own blood and fell forward trying to pull the knife out. He was dead immediately.

Wolf summoned Rabbit, who had brought plastic explosives and put them on the front door, as the rest of the team stood ready to storm the place as the door blow.

Badger saw it first through the scope of the sniper rifle General Fuentes saw it too with her night goggles. A figure of a person, dressed totally in black, had come out of nowhere and with an almost incredible jump, had reached the balcony, where Badger had just kill the guard. Two other figures, similarly clad and equally agile, followed the first one and entered the house.

Moose and Wolf had gone around the house in order to neutralize any men guarding the rear of the house. They found three guards, all dead with their throats sliced open.

"Somebody else is here, Commander. They may be helping us. They killed the guards in the back of the house."

"Then come to the front. Rabbit is ready to blow the door open. We will throw stun grenades. Hope we won't hit our friends."

Vince was still very groggy but had regained consciousness. Most likely he wasn't yet able to fully process what was going on, but Masters was eager to go ahead with his brutal and sinister plan. Two guys untied Kelly Carter and brought her to a table covered only with a dirty old mattress and started to rip off her clothes. She tried to scream with the little energy she had left.

With the corner of her good eye, she saw the walls moving and turning into people dressed in black, with faces covered and wielding samurai swords.

"Ninjas, I am dreaming of ninjas coming to rescue me. It must be a bucket wish."

Then she felt something worm and sticky spill over her and someone threw a ball near her. But the ball did not bounce and it had hair and then there was another hairy ball. It took her a moment to realize that the balls were the heads of the men who were going to rape her.

The people in black were bouncing off the floor, off the ceiling, off the furniture, off the walls, and each time their swords pierced someone's body or chopped off somebody's head.

Then there was an explosion and smoke filled the room. She heard two more explosions and then she passed out. The first explosion was the door being blown out, the other two stun grenades.

Of the seven ASP men who had been in the room, only

two were standing, General Masters and another man who moved into the back of the room and reached the next room as soon as the ninjas started killing his men. Therefore the stun grenades did not affect them as much.

There was a trap door in that room Masters opened and slid down into a tunnel, followed by the other man.

The stun grenades stun the Ninjas immobilizing them for a brief period of time and then they faced the gun yielding zoo squad. One of the Ninjas raised the hands and said in English, "We are friends, will not fight you."

"Okay, men," ordered Silvia, "put your weapons down. Go help Kelly and the others. Put a blanket of something over her and get her out of here while she is unconscious. I do not think it is healthy for her to see this carnage. Where is Masters? I do not see his body or his head here."

"Got away in a tunnel, but he won't go far. We know where he is going," said the Ninja.

"We need to capture him and turned over to the authorities; Wolf and Moose, go follow that tunnel."

"Sorry. We will get him first. It is Zhengyi for us". And the Ninja disappeared by jumping through the window.

Chapter 39
ZHENGYI

Wolf and Moose ran to the trap door and let themselves into the tunnel. They did not see any light at the end and neither saw Masters nor the other guy. However they kept pushing forward. The tunnel ended about one-third of the mile ahead where it opened into a hangar, where a four-seat, single-engine airplane was waiting.

Masters and his man ran ahead of Wolf and Moose, rapidly approaching the plane. Surprisingly, neither was running out of breath despite being past the age of 60.

Masters heard his companion say, "I guess we live to see another day boss. Where did all those people came from? They were like ghosts and moved like cats."

"Who knows? We will find out soon enough. Meanwhile, let's get out of here."

Masters climbed into the plane, and his man followed. Suddenly, the man fell backward. The only sound he made was his body hitting the floor of the hangar.

A Shuriken was deeply inserted on his neck, right at the base of the skull. Death had been instantaneous

Masters was surprised but still thinking that he could get away, got to the controls in the cockpit. This time he was surprised when a beautiful woman, with long black hair—and dressed completely in a black thigh jacket and pants—greeted him jokingly: "Welcome aboard air China general Masters, hope you will have a pleasant flight."

Masters tried to pull out his gun and retreat his steps to get out of the plane, but another Ninja put a knife on his neck and pressed it hard enough to cut the skin and draw some blood.

"Sit down, General, and be a good boy. My friend there would be very happy to slice your throat if you do not behave."

"Who are you people? How did you find this place? How

did you know that the tunnel ended in this hangar? Why did you murder all my men? Do you want money? I can pay you very handsomely if you land this plane where I was supposed to go…. How does a million dollars sound to you?"·

"Too many questions at the same time, General. You Americans are too inquisitive and think that money is the answer to every problem. "We are the Avengers or The Justice League. You ordered the murder of Doctor Ghan-Do and his wife, made her daughter an orphan, plotted to kill millions of mine and your people for money, and then escaped from American justice, which we do not trust anyway. Even if you did not escape, they would have treated you very leniently and probably end with just—what is the expression that you Americans use?—a slap on the wrist"

"I did not kill or order to kill the doctor and his family. I swear, I did not even know they had a daughter. It was the Russian guy, Leopold Mishanivich."

"Oh, yes, we know about him and will eventually find him. As to the second question, we followed your men after they kidnapped the Americans. Did a search to the area, found the plane, figured you would use it to get away and we waited for you here.

"We really did not want to kill your men. The plan was just to neutralize them and kill only if necessary, and then abduct you. But when we heard and saw what you were doing and going to do to that poor woman—some of my partners being women—could not control themselves. Those men deserved what they got and worse. Besides, they were all armed, probably had military training, and likely were stronger than us. And thank you, but we do not want your blood-stained money."

"You are all women?"

"More questions. Only a few of us are. The others are men. But enough questions. We are not here to chat with you."

Then she said something in Chinese to the other Ninja and he put a piece of duct tape on the mouth of the general and bound his arms and legs with more of it.

Wolf and Moose emerged from the tunnel only to see the plane taxing towards a runaway, ready to take off.

"Fuck, looks like he escaped again," said Moose.

"I am not so sure about that, Moose," Wolf said, pointing to the dead man lying on the floor.

They walked back to the main house, this time not through the tunnel.

"What a bloody mess," General Silvia Fuentes was saying. "We need to get Kelly, Vince, and the doctor to a hospital, but we cannot call the cops or an ambulance. There is no way we can explain or justify this massacre. We all did wear gloves, so make sure that we do not leave any trace of us being here. Badger, did you retrieve the spent cartridges of the sniper rifle? Yes, good! You men help the doctor and Vince to get their clothes on. I will cover Kelly with a blanket and we all will walk to the cars. We'll see if the Patels can drive the casualties to the hospital. They are the only ones that can be seen and interrogated without a problem."

Wolf and Moose were back and reported that the Ninjas had taken Masters with them on an airplane, emphasizing that he most likely did not escape justice.

Vince and Doctor Thurston were conscious and alert but in a lot of pain. Both probably had broken ribs and the doctor was developing some difficulty breathing, indicating that a broken rib may be piercing his lung. Vince had a killer headache and was a little lightheaded, but both understood that the story they were going to tell the authorities was that they were kidnapped and tortured. Then some group of people stormed the place and there was a fight.

While that fight took place, they saw the opportunity to get away. They walked to the main road and were picked up by the Patels, who were driving by.

Kelly was still in a daze. She probably would not remember much.

As they were walking away towards their vehicles, they saw that the drones that were under the vehicles of Master's men had come alive again, were flying away towards the forest, and disappeared.

Meanwhile the airplane carrying the now helpless General Masters had taken off and was hovering at low altitude over the woods. The pilot was talking over the radio with someone in the ground. They were speaking English, in case someone could pick up their frequency.

"That was not in the plans. Why did you take the plane?" the voice on the ground asked.

"Sorry, we had to improvise. We were being followed and the main package was already on board, attempting to get away."

"So, what are you going to do now? Where will you be landing that thing?"

"Thinking about it. The plane is small. It could land on a street or a parking lot."

"Like the second option best. Land at the mall where we left the vehicles. All the shops will be closing now. Meet you there in forty-five minutes. Burn some fuel. No further communications, over."

The woman flew the small plane over the woods in circles for about half an hour, then headed to the strip mall, hoping that the parking lot would be empty.

The parking lot was indeed empty and well lit. She knew the only vehicles parked there belonged to her team. One was a big truck in which the ATVs were transported, another was a Hummer, and a third was a van with electronic equipment.

She cut the engine off and took the plane almost into a dive until it was just above the level of the roofs of the buildings near the mall. Then, gently, she put the plane at one end of the parking lot and taxied it to almost the other end, where it stopped completely.

The woman and the other Ninja pushed the bound Master unceremoniously through the door and he landed about six feet below on the hard pavement. Four other men came and carried Masters to the van. The woman rode shotgun in a Hummer, which was driven by another woman just as gorgeous as the first.

"It was a lot of excitement for one day, sis, wasn't it?" she said.

"You are nuts, cousin," the other one responded Both laughed.

The FBI had raided the ASP headquarters two days earlier, taking computers and files with them but making no arrests and, so far, nobody had been indicted. Yet, the doors of the main building remained temporarily sealed with yellow tape.

Yet, two days later, the police found that the tapes from the entrance to the main ASP building had been mysteriously removed, the crystal of the front door broken and suspended from a chandelier. Just steps from the entrance, the body of a man was hanging. The man was naked from the waist up; across his chest and forehead, the word ZHENGYI was written.

The forensics later determined that the words had not been written. They had been branded, letter by letter, with a hot iron, and ZHENGYI was the Chinese word for justice.

The body of the hanged man belonged to General Charles Flynn Masters.

The official cause of death, released to the press by the police and the government, was suicide.

Masters had no next of kin. Having been married and divorced twice, had two grown-up kids with the first wife and none with the second. Both women were dead now. The kids lived in Japan and had no contact with their father in years.

Masters would be buried alone, neither the President nor the Vice-President attended.

The morning TV news was busy reporting that some nut had landed a plane in a shopping center parking lot in the middle of the night. The FBI identified it as the plane where Masters had escaped.

Evidently, the general did not make it to the Bahamas.

Chapter 40
CLOSING THE BOOK

As soon as the media gave the news, the stock of ASP dropped from the forty-four dollars it was trading at to a meager four dollars. Many employees of the company abandoned their jobs and disappeared overnight.

The remaining four of the main stockholders attempted to leave the country but were arrested by the FBI, as they had been specifically told not to do that.

Mr. Jason White's lawyer visited them in jail and offered to buy their shares, buildings, and all assets of ASP for six million dollars. The offer dropped by half a million every day that they waited to agree to the sale. In the end, Mr. White paid only one-and-a-half million dollars for something worth twenty times as much.

Mr. Jason White's representative also visited Karla Messer (aka the Lioness) and paid her the amounts of money that she had put into the operation, plus a hefty interest. They talked her into leasing her cabin in the woods temporarily as headquarters for the team to occupy until the FBI gave the okay to move into the main campus of ASP. It was now the property of Mr. White, who was offering them, a salary with benefits, plus a share in the stock of the company, as long as they were willing to work there as employees, although eventually they would be regarded as executives with a share of the profits of the company. It was suggested that the name ASP be preserved, as the name was known to employers and clients with which the company still had many legal contracts. The Patel cousins, who by then were considered part of the team, were in charge of electronic surveillance and internet protection.

Of course, Jason White was not the monetary provider for most of the money for the takeover. It was the senator, who, for obvious reasons, preferred that his name would not be involved, but was in equal partnership with his bodyguard and friend. The Senator began considering running for President of the United States.

Doctor Thurston had to have a chest tube to drain the air leaking out of his lung, which had been perforated by a broken rib. He endured five days of hospitalization, during which the FIB and Homeland Security frequently interrogated him. He continued to stick to the story of being kidnapped and taken to a place where Mrs. Carter was also being held and tortured. He had been beaten badly, so he was semi-conscious when he heard an explosion and shots being fired. Then, someone cut the duct tape he was bound with and he took the opportunity to escape, dragging Mrs. Carter along with the help of Lieutenant Batagliari who had been beaten worse than him. No, he was not sure how they got to the main road; perhaps the people who freed them helped, but neither one of the three of them remembered that clearly.

Vince Batagliari was discharged after twenty-four hours, still with a killer headache but reassured that the CAT scan of his head was normal.

Kelly Carter was not as lucky because, in addition to facial and head contusions, she had a cerebral concussion and a severe psychological shock. She had no memory of the events, even after she spent a week in the hospital and a full month in a rehabilitation facility, after which she moved to Florida to live with her parents.

The narrative given to the media was that Mrs. Carter had escaped her captors with the help of her friends Dr. Joe Thurston and Lieutenant Vincenso Batagliari, who had also been kidnapped. Because they all had received multiple head traumas, they were unable to tell where they had been held, although they did say that General Masters was the leader of their captors.

The media and the paparazzi hounded them for days with silly questions like, "How did you feel about being tortured?". "Did it hurt much? "Did you think you were going to die?".

Thurston answered with irritation and scorn: "It wasn't pleasant." "Yes, it hurt a lot." "Yes, we thought we were going to die."

Obviously, Kelly was in no shape to be interviewed. Vince, still with a headache, had one of those "events." He called the reporters stupid, punched one, and broke the camera of another before being subdued by hospital security.

On a separate note, a small report on the back pages of the local paper it was reported that "a shooting between gangs involved in human trafficking left several gang members dead at a rural Virginia farm." It said that the FBI had not been able to identify the weapons used because they found none.

A couple of days later, Senator McClain received an invitation to lunch with the Chinese Ambassador.

When they met at an expensive Oriental restaurant, Senator McClain was surprised to see that the Ambassador was accompanied by a woman of astonishing beauty: hair black as a raven's feathers, worn casually to shoulder length, framing a perfect face, jade green oriental eyes, with long, sensual eyelashes, a small mouth, with just a touch of pink rouge, a slender neck on which she wore a gold necklace with tiny pieces of Jade dangling from it, each representing one of the animals of the Chinese calendar. She wore a black thigh-cut dress, which was not too short, not too long, just a bit below her knee, enough to show a gorgeous pair of legs. It ended at small feet, on which she wore the tallest and pointiest heels that the senator had ever seen. The woman moved graciously and sensually, at times resembling the movements of a cat.

The Ambassador apologized to the Senator for bringing along an unexpected guest, whom he introduced simply as Miss Lee, the daughter of a good friend. The Chinese Ambassador explained that Miss Lee's father had insisted that she come along and he believed that McClain would be pleased, not only for sharing a meal with such a beautiful lady but also interested in what she had to say. Apparently, Miss Lee, if that was her real name, did not speak English, so the Ambassador was to translate.

After recovering from the surprise and after the usual formalities, the Senator said to his companions.

"Thank you for the invitation, Mr. Ambassador; I came

here thinking that we were just to have an interesting lunch during which you were going to tell me that your government has the virus and where, and instead, you bring along a beauty queen, a real movie star."

The Ambassador just smiled and said, "Come on, Senator, you know that my government was not even aware of the existence of that virus. As soon as we learned about it, the laboratory was dismantled. The scientists who worked on it were arrested, put to trial and many were sent to prison. Of course, we will keep the vaccines, just in case they are needed in a future day.

"But enough of that, Senator. The subject may be too boring to the lady. Better order something to eat."

They ordered Chinese beer, except for Ms. Lee, who only ordered tea. The three had fish. They ate, maintaining a mundane conversation, with the Ambassador translating to the woman. At the end of the meal, the men ordered coffee, and the lady just water with a twist of lemon; the Ambassador said:

"Before we say goodbye, Miss. Lee wants to present the Senator with a gift as a token of friendship from her father," he said while handling the senator an envelope.

"Sorry, please tell Miss Lee that I do not take bribes," and he got up, ready to leave.

"Please sit, Senator. It is not money. It is something that you may find interesting and useful. Please open it."

The senator sat down again and opened the envelope, which contained several photographs of two police officers, some of the pictures showing them carrying an unconscious person. There was also a cell phone in the envelope.

"What is this, Ambassador?" McClain inquired.

"Those, sir, are the photos of the two guys who, posing as police officers, killed two real cops and almost killed an FBI operative. Mr. Lee thinks you may find those pictures useful. Now, if you please turn on the cell phone and play the video."

McClain did and saw that the video recorded the events before the Ninja attack on Masters and his gang. It clearly showed Kelly, with her clothes torn and face bruised and swollen, and Masters kicking Dr. Thurston and Vincenso. But more shocking was hearing Masters telling his men what he was going to do to Kelly. The video ended as she was about to be raped. Of course, he guessed what happened next, as General Fuentes-Graham had reported to him about the Ninjas.

"Oh, my God," said the Senator, "that fucken son of a bitch Masters deserved everything that came to him. Please do not translate that to the lady."

The policemen in the pictures were two of the ASP executives, right now in FBI custody.

"How did you or Mr. Lee obtain these?"

"Oh, my Dear Senator, the American eagle is very powerful. She can fly very high and her eyes can see very far. But the dragon has many eyes and also can fly very high."

"What does Mr. Lee want in exchange for these? Would you ask her?"

"Miss Lee tells me that her father does not want anything in exchange, only your friendship. However, he will appreciate it very much if you could tell him where Leopold Mishanivich is, the Russian operative."

"Why does he think that I know anything about that person"?

"Senator, do I have to remind you that dragons have many eyes?"

The senator did not feel very comfortable giving information to these Chinese. However, the information that they had given him was very valuable, and Leopold was a scum bag, almost as bad as Masters, and he had escaped punishment. And he had done so with his help.

"All I can tell Mr. Lee, because it is all I know, is that the guy is in Mexico, probably Ciudad Juarez."

"Thank you, Senator, that is helpful. It was nice to have lunch with you. However, remember that we never had this conversation."

"Likewise, Mr. Ambassador"

"You should run for President, Senator McClain. You will have our support."

"Sorry, thank you, but I cannot accept foreign aid. Thank you for offering".

"Not even from a beautiful woman from New York?" Miss Lee said in perfect English while blowing him a kiss as she was leaving.

The Senator had to sit down again and thought to himself, "OMG, I think I just had lunch with the most beautiful Ninja in the whole world."

POTUS left the White House after being impeached but was never indicted of any criminal activity related to the murders, the riots, or plotting to kill millions with a deathly virus. The main reason was that neither Congress, lawyers, nor even the Supreme Court could determine whether the pardon that he had given himself protected him from prosecution. He retired to his penthouse on Park Avenue, New York, and tried to write his memoirs.

However, his trophy wife divorced him, took a big chunk of the multiple millions that he had, and actually wrote a book herself, which turned out to be a best-seller, making her a few more million as it was in the New York best-seller for a month.

Nevertheless, POTUS was very rich, still had several million left, and had a good number of adorers around the country, people who firmly believed that he had been given a proverbial coup d'état. He was invited to speak at major Universities for hefty fees. However, that did not last because one day, or perhaps one night, a few months after the so-called, suicide of the general, a picture of Masters hanging from the chandelier and with the word ZHENGYI clearly shown across his chest was found pinned to the headboard of his bed.

After that, the ex-President developed a serious case of paranoia, which worsened over the following months and years, to the point that he would not want to leave the penthouse, even when accompanied by bodyguards. Psychiatrists and therapists gave him all kinds of medications, but his paranoia impeded him from taking them, believing that the doctors were in a plot to poison him.

Percy D. Kepfer

Two years later his fears became real, as he fell from the balcony of his penthouse to the street. His death was also regarded as suicide, though some hobo sleeping on the sidewalk across the street swore that he saw a black shadow pushing him down.

Almost nobody believed the poor guy.

The ex-Vice-President bought a ranch in Montana, raised fine-breed horses, and stopped practicing law. But he assisted local lawyers, pro bono, in defending people with no financial recourses. He declined multiple invitations to speak at colleges and universities.

Also, about two years later, he was found dead in the stall of his favorite horse. Apparently, he had been kicked and trampled by the stallion.

Thanks to the evidence presented by Senator McClain to the FBI, The ASP operatives who kidnapped Kelly Carter were charged with double, premeditated murder, attempted murder, kidnapping, and several other charges and given three life sentences to be served consecutively and no possibility of parole.

The two others were given ten years as accessories, but neither completed it as one really committed suicide, and the other died of a coronary attack. Both were in their early sixties.

Senator McClain became very popular and launched a campaign to run for President with a good chance of being elected.

Kelly Carter, who had become a schoolteacher in Florida, helped him run his campaign in the Sunshine State. Although she was never quite the same as before her ordeal, she always said that she had no regrets and was proud of what she did.

After being granted a full pardon and restoration of their military ranks and pensions, The Zoo team resigned from the military and went to work for the ASP Corporation.

After weeding out many shoddy previous contracts, ASP started getting new, legal ones and was making money. In less than a year, shares were trading at fifteen bucks.

Doctor Joe Thurston remained the team physician. They

all realized that the problems related to the serum's effects were easy to manage when they were together and supporting each other, just like AA.

It helped that they finally agreed to take the medications that Dr. Thurston had discovered to help the best their impulse control: a mixture of tiny doses of lithium and Guanfacine.

The one with the most difficulty was Badger, who had to fight his many demons. But eventually, he stopped drinking or using drugs.

There was only one problem: nobody really liked the moniker "Zoo team," and it was difficult to reach a consensus on a new name. Wolf, who was the leader in the absence of Silvia. She was allowed to call the shots as number one of the team. General Silvia was also a partner of ASP.

Wolf suggested that the team should be called THE HOMELESS SQUAD since everyone had been homeless at one time or another. General Silvia Fuentes—Graham approved, and this name was unanimously accepted.

One day, after checking his e-mail, Rabbit excitedly announced, "Hey fellows, we have the first job as the Homeless Squad. A Chinese fellow wants us to track down Leopold in Mexico. The payment they offer is incredible."

The matter was to be discussed at the next ASP meeting.

General Silvia Fuentes-Graham, who had not been in a serious relationship since the death of her husband, Sergeant Mayor Keith Graham, a few years earlier in Afghanistan, accepted the invitation of Dr. Joe Thurston to take a trip together to tour the major European cities for a month.

She gladly accepted.

THE END

www.ingramcontent.com/pod-product-compliance
Lightning Source LLC
Chambersburg PA
CBHW070926250626
47159CB00009B/3143